Book One The Courthouse Series

DETENTION

Carolyn Marks Johnson

Production Manager: Kimberly Verhines

ISBN: 978-1-62288-261-8

For more information:
Stephen F. Austin State University Press
P.O. Box 13007 SFA Station
Nacogdoches, Texas 75962
sfapress@sfasu.edu
936-468-1078

Distributed by the Texas A&M University Press Book Consortium
www.tamupress.com

This legal romance is dedicated to my mother, Jacqueline Thomas Marks, who became the legal guardian of her seven brothers and sisters in the GREAT DEPRESSION and kept her family together by taking-in sewing. She was the most talented, smartest, most trusted and the strongest woman I ever knew. She gave a strong work ethic to her siblings and her own six children.

ACKNOWLEDGMENTS:

DETENTION and RUTTER INDUSTRIES would not have been possible without the support of Dr. Beverly Parker, who gave them each close reading, and to my legal team of Barbara Baruch, attorney, and the Honorable John Ackerman, retired District Judge for the State of Texas. These three people have been my life-time friends.

DETENTION: The Act of keeping back, of withholding, either accidentally or by design, a person or thing . . .

DETENTION HEARING: Judicial or quasi-judicial proceeding used to determine the propriety of detaining a person on bail or a juvenile in a shelter facility.[1]

---

1   Henry Campbell Black, M.A. *Black's Law Dictionary, Definition of the Terms and phrases of American and English Jurisprudence, Ancient and Modern,* 5th Ed. West Publishing, St. Paul, Minn. 1979.

CONTENTS

PART TWO

Part I

CHAPTER ONE:
The Detention Center

"Trust me, girlfriend," I tell my new client. "You're in a heap of trouble."

I shake out a pair of the Detention Center's folded coveralls. They are wrinkled and stiff, but freshly washed, and give off a faint aroma of soap.

"What's your name, honey?" I know it, but she's been so out of it, she's barely known her own name for the last few hours.

"Fee-bee" She answers.

"Mine's Shadow. Here, help me get this on you."

"No! Not on my body," she insists. "Give me my clothes and I will dress myself." She enunciates each syllable.

I look over at Evie Lane, the supervisor of female deputies for the county. She is in the holding cell with me and the girl.

"Let's just let her have her clothes back," I say.

Betsy Moore, a rookie deputy starting a public service career at forty, pulls a chair into the hallway. She seems overly enthusiastic about her new line of work, like she doesn't want to miss how Evie handles this.

Felipe "Fee Lo" Hernandez, the Deputy Chief of the Center, hovers near the entrance of the block of 8 x 8-foot barred cells, but does not come into the block to maintain the girl's privacy.

"No," Evie says. "Can't do that. No bra and no panties until we have a better idea of her mental state."

Evie knows what she is doing and is following standard procedure. If this young woman was really in danger, she would already have called an ambulance to take her to the hospital. Evie is an expert at dealing with drunk and drugged kids.

"My mental state is fine," the girl says with surprising clarity for her condition.

Phoebe seems overwhelmed by that brief effort to declare normalcy and sits, still naked and defiant. Thin is an understatement with this child. Only sixteen, she looks to be about a hundred pounds, with her bones sticking out everywhere. She still refuses to cover even the most private parts of her pale and sickly-looking body.

"You're the boss," I tell Evie.

"And you know the rules, Miss McLeod"

"Call me Shadow," I say as if irritated. I shrug and look back at Phoebe, hoping to establish some kind of rapport that will open an avenue of communication, but she is still scowling at all of us. *Typical teenager*, I think.

Evie sighs. "My experience with these kids is that when they get in deep trouble, they can't handle it. They are kids, after all."

"And I suspect a kid who blows away another kid with a close-up, heartfelt gunshot wound to the face..." I sigh and shake my head. "...will probably go apeshit when she comes off the high and reality sinks in."

I approach Phoebe again. She seems slightly calmer.

"We are going to make this work," I tell her, leaning in close until she looks me in the eye.

"I don't want a lawyer," she says in return. "I want you to call my grandfather this minute." Her words are still slurred but she enunciates as much as she can to emphasize her dismissal of me.

"The judge appointed me," I tell her.

"You don't even look like a lawyer," she says with a sneer. I give myself a once-over. Hair a mess. Leggings. T-shirt. Jacket. No bra. Low boots. A faint giggle escapes from Evie, who probably thinks the same thing. They're not wrong, either.

"You have a point," I say. "I sure don't have on my jury-picking skirt and heels. But it is three in the morning, and I didn't have a lot of time."

She shrugs and grimaces, leaning away from me. "Just go away."

"I will," I say. "As soon as we have your hearing. Come on now, let's get you dressed. You're going to meet the judge."

"No!"

"This isn't negotiable, Phoebe. The law says we have to do this."

Through the window, which is just barely at eye level, barred and
apparently unopenable, I see the Center's gate open. The razor-wire
slinky on top of the gate sends reflected pinpricks of light through the
darkness. The gate stays open just long enough to allow a small gray Prius to enter. It does not give access to a pick-up truck with absurdly large
tires behind it. After the gate closes, the little car's driver steers around
County-issued sedans and pick-ups until he finds a space and steps out
of the car, locking it and standing, waiting, until the headlights go out.

I recognize Judd Baker, one of the judges who presides over cases at the Center. He balances his briefcase and an oversized McDon-
ald's coffee cup as he picks his way through a path that skirts the cars
but also cuts between two seesaws and a jungle gym. The playground
equipment is placed prominently, as if the Center hopes to fool the
world into thinking it's a school. Despite these small concessions to
the look of freedom, liberty, and child welfare, the Center is a jail. It
is a prison for children, not any fancier than the ones serving adults.

"Judge Baker just drove up," I say. Fee Lo—that is, Deputy Hernandez—remains outside the block and Evie takes up the center of
the small cell. She stands firmly, ready to get this child dressed one
way or another. Ordinarily, the hearing might wait for a more decent
hour, but Fee Lo made the call to ask the Judge to come to the Center.
He wants to dot the i's and cross the t's on this one, which has already
caught the attention of the press.

Betsy goes to let the judge in.

Evie holds out the coveralls and shakes them, stirring the air. One
end of the steel-barred cell sports a small stainless-steel toilet, which
like the cot is bolted to the concrete block wall. The far wall provides
the only color in the room, a pale green. At the other end, a metal sink
holds a roll of toilet paper doing double duty as paper towels, a wad of
which has been pulled out and laid over something on the floor. It's not
difficult to tell that this is where the heavy stench is coming from: the
girl must have thrown up right before I got here.

"She's been throwing up off and on since she started coming
down from whatever she was on. Withdrawal's a bitch." Evie says.
The mingled smells in the small cell are almost enough to make me
nauseous. I know they clean with some liquid cleanser that I see them

spraying all the time since the pandemic, but it can't hide that burning bleach scent, which will be trapped in my nose for a couple days.

When Phoebe was brought in, sometime within the last 48 hours, they dressed her in the standard issue coveralls and took her bra, panties, and street clothes so there was no chance of her harming herself with them once she came out of her drug-induced delirium. Had she been unconscious they might have taken her to the nearest hospital. But she wasn't, just doped up and angry about being in a cell. When she started to come down from the high, the first thing she did was rip off the coveralls and throw them across the cell. She then started demanding that they call her Grandfather. Evie and Betsy have been trying to get her dressed since.

"Come on, kid." I say to Phoebe. "Please. We need to get you dressed. You're going to see the judge tonight."

"No," she says, shaking her head. Her short dark haircut is swinging around, spiky blonde highlights moving in a wild fury. Her quiet, passive state is transitioning into agitation and lashing out as whatever drugs had been in her system continue to wear off.

"Yes!" I say, stepping over to where Fee Lo waits so I can talk to him between the bars.

"Help me out here," I ask him. "At least give me a heads up before I have to face the judge with her. Why the stubborn refusal to listen to anybody? Why the refusal to even pretend she's done something wrong? She's mad at us, as if we're the ones overreacting here."

"She's a MacPearson," he says. "I should have told you, but I was afraid you wouldn't be willing to help." He directs his voice more toward Phoebe than me. "I know how you feel about little rich kids that do what they please. But I can't make her poor and deserving. She is what she is. I've had her here before, more than once. I don't think she's a bad person, but she's one of the most neglected kids I've ever seen."

I look carefully at him. He's playing me and I know it. We've worked together enough times for him to know about my weakness for the kind of kids who end up in the Center. Most of the kids I see here have never had a break and won't ever get one, even from us most of the time.

"We managed to get in touch with her mother, but she's refused to come," Fee Lo tells me, voice lowered. He's not trying to reach

Phoebe anymore, now he's trying to persuade me. "She actually accepted the State's argument that Phoebe should be certified tonight to be tried as an adult."

"She doesn't want her to be tried here?" This is different from other kids I've worked with. This kid's mom has no idea about the realities of life if she really wants her kid to be treated like an adult in a real courthouse, and not here where she has a little more constitutional protection.

"She refuses to come here to this '*concrete box.*'"

"Crazy spoiled bitch." I reply, matching Fee Lo's quiet tone. A part of me can see the mom's motivation, because I do love working in a real courthouse. The older, the better. Some of those old brick and stone piles are the most beautiful buildings in the state, standing like a monument to the law in the center of a town.

Detention Centers often do not look like courthouses. Most, like this one, are square concrete block boxes and corrogated steel walls in a fenced yard. Some have decorative open gates to suggest freedom, but Detention Centers lock up the same as any jail. The inmates might be younger, but they're definitely not free to leave.

Phoebe's mother, part of the MacPearson family, probably never worked a day in her life. I can't help but compare her with the good parents who do their best but are prevented from being there for their children These parents simply can't come out here because they don't have a car or will lose their job if they take off to attend their child's hearing. Phoebe's mother, with all the privileges of wealth and influence, can't be bothered to even visit, much less pay for a lawyer or send comfortable clothing that might help her child get through this.

I haven't even agreed to take Phoebe's case yet, and I could walk away now if I wanted to. Fee Lo knows this…but he also knows what a sucker I am for a neglected kid who doesn't have anyone in her corner. He gives me a look as if to say that he already knows how invested I am in this kid, then steps into the cell and past me to talk to Phoebe. The cell suddenly feels very small, and the smell of bleach is making my head swim.

"Maybe you should just admit that we failed," I tell Fee Lo, "and give up. You got me out here. She doesn't want me to be her lawyer. Just lock her up and call somebody tomorrow."

Fee Lo speaks calmly, ignoring Phoebe's shaking head, thrashing arms, and naked thinness to look her in the eyes. "I don't have another lawyer that I can call at 3:30 in the morning. We need to get Phoebe dressed. Evie?"

Instead of being calmed, the girl kicks him on his shin.

I see the grimace. It had to be painful.

"My bad," he says. "Didn't mean to get in your space, Phoebe." His eyes narrow and his voice drops. I know the signs of his anger when he's had enough. The girl also takes notice too, a wary look on her face.

"Understand, Phoebe," he says. "I'm not saying the judge will even consider letting you go home. This is a serious case. But you can't even go in there to see the judge without clothes and if you can't go in there, he can't do anything for you. The choice is yours."

Instead of calming down, she kicks Evie.

"Hey!" I command. "Stop that! Kicking the deputy is another felony charge—you really want to add a third degree felony to the first degree felony charge you've already got?"

She kicks in my direction but Evie grabs her and holds her arms tightly by her side, lifting her feet off the floor.

"Honey, I don't like this any better than you do, but if you make me, I will have them hold you down to dress you and cuff you before we go in to see the judge. If that's what you want the judge to see, then keep kicking."

I dare to reach out and run my hand over this skinny little girl's hair, smoothing down the tangles that have formed from all her shaking. She looks startled, then relaxes momentarily.

"You haven't done that in years," she whispers and lets Evie pull the coveralls over her bony legs. She stands quietly when prompted as the woman tugs the wrinkled coveralls over her arms. I step back and watch Evie get her ready. Phoebe's head felt so awkward in my hand, but somebody important to her must have done that before. It must have been a long, long time ago if Fee Lo is right and her anger is also fueled by neglect.

Evie gives me a sidelong glance and smiles as she pulls the darker blue paper footies onto the girl's feet, taking advantage of her momentary cooperation.

"Wow. This kid took or was given a butt-load of something," Evie says, as the girl sits back down, apparently exhausted from the simple effort of standing for a few minutes. She remains still though as Evie rolls up the excess fabric at her wrists and ankles. This child really is tiny.

"We gotta find your feet in there, girl," Evie says with a mock struggle to finally uncover the ankles.

"I'm so tired," Phoebe says and tries to lie back on the cot with a mattress as mashed flat as a yoga pad.

"Can't do that now," I say. "Judge is waiting."

We can hear Betsy and the judge greet each other and discuss the case file, which is apparently on his computer. Evie and I easily support Phoebe between us and head out for the courtroom. As Evie and I walk the girl down the hallway, I tell her Miss Evie once took down a 200 pound male resister all on her own: we all got out of her way. Evie is one strong and tough lady. But I get no response from the child. I am beginning to hope that when she comes out of this state, I'll be able to connect with her beyond just feeling sorry for her. I know that Evie and Fee Lo and even newcomer Betsy are only here because they are committed to helping the kids, even those that don't seem to want to be helped.

I notice sometimes that these two women, Evie and Betsy, are as protective of their Deputy as I am. Both have admitted that they thought I was trying to get something going with Fee Lo when I first started coming out here to work, a couple of years ago. I've never been one of his (many) women; they know that now. Truthfully, I do love that little bastard. We've worked together on several intense cases that could have made us enemies, but instead have made us friends. I know our closeness has generated the usual courthouse gossip, but there's never been anything to it. We probably couldn't ever get together at this point, since we have such a great working relationship and friendship. I wouldn't take a chance of wasting that on sex!

We are very close, though. He taught me how to drive his Harley, and he's very open with me. Even though we've only known each other a couple of years, we know more about each other than some people that we have known all our lives. It comes from all those evenings sitting in the hot tub talking things over, drinking beer for him and Pinot Grigio for me and talking trash.

I have watched how the kids who come here automatically look up to Fee Lo and do what he says. I don't know how he does it; but there's no denying his charisma and their attachment. My client, little Phoebe, may be the sole exception that I've seen. Even in her drug-induced confusion, she obviously respects no one. Nor does she appreciate the finer aspects or protections of her current location, here in the Detention Center.

She is a MacPearson, as Fee Lo said. As we walk slowly toward the makeshift courtroom, stopping frequently so Phoebe can lean on one of us and rest, I learn about where some of her anger is coming from. She asks to talk to her grandfather several times and gets more and more agitated with each refusal. She seems to think that if she could just talk to him, he would come take her home, as if she weren't in the Center because of a violent crime.

The hearing probably won't take long, partly because it is about 3:30 in the morning. I'm only here so that Phoebe can have a lawyer present when appearing before this District Court Judge, who will be doing a probable cause inquiry. The question the Judge or Magistrate must answer: *Is there evidence sufficient to hold her in jail for conduct that violates a law?*

And, yes, I would say, the State can show probable cause here. The investigating sheriff wrote that in a gathering of friends, Phoebe walked in on her best friend in Phoebe's bed with her drug-dealing boyfriend, took a gun from her bedside table, and shot the girl in the face, with some thirty other juveniles as witnesses. I'd call that sufficient cause for Phoebe to be held at no bail.

The Constitution and law require that a judge, or someone with authority such as a magistrate, decide the answer to that question within 48 hours of an arrest and then set an appropriate bond, if the accused is eligible. Since she's taken more than 24 hours to come down from whatever was in her system, this hearing is pretty time sensitive. Given what she is accused of and her current state, there's no question of the result of the inquiry. Given who she is, Fee Lo was right to call out this retired district court judge to arraign her and a lawyer to represent her so she can know fully what she is facing.

A "Detention Center" sounds a little bit like being in school, like being sent by the teacher to a chair at the back of a classroom, but the Detention process is serious business. A child can end up with a life sentence, though a minor can no longer be executed since 2005, even for such things as murder.

Phoebe doesn't seem to appreciate any of the legal protections she is receiving at this time. She asks again and again for her grandfather and seems angry that we have not called him to take her home. Grandpa has been called and he's not here! Phoebe may be about to get a taste of reality. If the Judge holds her tonight, they have to visit the same topic in ten days. So she can be here for a while, not just a night!

Her grandfather is *Bull* MacPearson, the grand old man of the county. He holds the elected office of County Judge, a political position heading up the County's Board of Commissioners. As far as I know, no one has ever filed charges against him for anything dishonest: most people consider him a funny old guy. In recent years, he's become known for using the wrong name to address visitors to the county and malapropping words. He blames these blunders on too many tackles when he was a Houston Oiler running back. "Getting hit and hitting back harder wearing leather helmets," he'll say in explanation.

Most people find him charming. His son and his son's recently divorced wife, they don't find charming. Like their daughter, Phoebe, both parents are only children of about four born-on-the-island families accustomed to getting their way, however much it upsets the rest of mankind.

But, in person, sliding her dark blue paper footies over the tile floor, their daughter looks very vulnerable. Evie and I are holding her up to make sure she doesn't fall while walking into the courtroom. And whether it is this dependency or the fact she looks sickly and pale, she does not look like anything that could kill another person in cold blood.

Having had a chance to look at Phoebe's file, I'm feeling a bit better about the situation. She has one prior from about two years ago—shoplifting from the Neiman's in Houston—but is clean otherwise. The biggest concern in the file is a note about possible suspicious behavior with her boyfriend, Henry "Ace" Tuttle, the main

witness to her alleged crime. Her boyfriend was the high school football star who flamed out after graduating high school. Apparently he
was busted a couple of times for being on the high school campus. He
was supposedly only there to visit his underage girlfriend, though as
a known dealer, he was almost certainly there to push drugs.

Hopefully when Phoebe becomes more alert, she'll have some
more details for me about what happened. I need some answers so
that I can give her an appropriate defense when the time comes.
Sometimes, when I get a new case such as this one, it appears there
is no good defense. It's going to be a hard time denying that she did
it. She needs treatment. Phoebe is a teen in need of supervision if
anyone ever were. Thirty other kids—allegedly—saw it go down.
Maybe that's something I can use. The sobriety of those thirty alleged
witnesses was in the sheriff's report: 'all were drunk and disorderly.'

She certainly wasn't sober either. But although intoxication is not
a defense, how she got that way may be. I make a mental note to look
at the other evidence from the sheriff's interviews with the kids at the
party. I need to find out what these kids had to say about Phoebe and
her older, dealing boyfriend.

"Poppi'll get me out," Phoebe says, almost like a warning, her
words backed by the certainty of a teenager used to getting her way.

Not tonight, Miss Phoebe, I think; *Nobody is getting you out of
here, honey,* I want to tell her. But I don't.

"Home," she whines piteously and attempts to collapse into the
chair as she did on the cot in her cell. But Evie and I still have hold
of an arm each and keep her from doing a swan dive in front of the
judge. We lower her into the chair by the small table that has been set
aside for the juvenile and her counsel. Evie grabs another chair from
the row at the back of the room and installs herself at the end of the
table. This small room is what passes for a courtroom in the Detention Center, but at least juveniles have their own space.

"Where is the State?" she asks me.

"William Catherton Bennett was here earlier," I say.

"I'll bet he's still asleep," she says and leaves us long enough
to whisper something to Fee Lo. He gets up and disappears into the
back room.

Meanwhile, the judge, a retired District Court Judge considered to be one of the greats, quietly comes into the courtroom ahead of us and takes his seat. He looks about as if he's not quite sure who to address.

I stand.

"Alexandra McLeod for the juvenile, Phoebe Sunshine MacPearson, Your Honor."

"Any word from the State?"

"We think he's on the way, Your Honor."

"Let's be at ease then," the judge says. He looks around, almost in dismay, and I know what he's thinking. The first time I saw this courtroom, I also found it strange. It's not a normal-looking courtroom; it's a square box they put a few basic fixtures in to allow the work to be done, but there are no polished extras. A rudimentary bench sits awkwardly in front of the judge's chair, which is the nicest piece of furniture in the room. While the bench has room for the clerks, they usually sit to one side in chairs against the wall. The court reporter takes the other side, and any witnesses sit in chairs to the side of the bench, facing the Judge.

Judd Baker's look in my direction almost compels a response, but I say nothing. I've gotten used to this place, but I can still see it may need some window dressing for newcomers. An older lawyer asked me once in this same room: "What's a nice girl like you doing in a place like this?"

"I admit the place hardly looks all that impressive," I told him with a smile. "But I like the work."

The old lawyer just patted my shoulder in the same way my mother does to allow lesser people to know she knows best. Just like that elderly lawyer, my mother sometimes looks at me like she wants to say: "Poor girl," or some such put-down. My mother would be happier if I carried a briefcase for one of the famous lawyers in our semi-metropolitan area until I become famous myself. She always wanted a high-profile kid.

I've heard that young lawyers avoid juvenile work because they think being assigned to work at the Detention Center is like being sent to legal reform school for new lawyers. The County Commissioners, who provide most of the funding for the juvenile courts, have been quoted before saying things like: '*it takes too much of the county's money to molly-coddle little hoodlums while they mature to become full-fledged criminals.*'

I read an article recently that claimed parents resent Detention Centers as '*interfering with their ability to control their own children.*' Those parents are simply wrong. Poor parenting is often the reason these kids are in trouble in the first place! While it's the court's job to make sure these kids receive appropriate consequences for their illegal actions, it's my job to make sure they have someone in their corner. Almost every day I get the chance to feel I made life better for a kid, even if they don't always know enough about the trouble they're in to appreciate it.

There are two judges who take turns on the juvenile docket. Judge Tamara Brown loves kids and is content with her work here at the Detention Center. The other, Lilly Pruser, is miserable here and wants a higher court. Judge Baker is sitting for Judge Pruser while she visits her ailing mother.

I know that everyone who works here at the Center likes to think that they have the juveniles' best interests at heart all the time, that we're really making a difference. The kids have their hearings right here in this somewhat dismal place, and then appear before a judge at least every ten days if there are delays in the process. But for many, even when they are allowed to go home, no home wants to take them back. Parents can refuse to allow their kids back into the home during that horrible period of limbo after the juvenile has been charged but before the kid is proved to have engaged in deliquent conduct. They can end up in the foster system or on the streets, surviving on street sex and hand-outs.

The justice system for kids often doesn't protect the kids who need protection most. When parents refuse the return of a child, Detention Centers become what they really are: prisons. Hallways are carved into cell blocks of locked-down, barred cells, with doors that close to that wretched complaint of metal striking metal.

That sound is what those kids live with.

All in all, Detention Centers are misfits. They are courts but don't look like it. They try hard not to look like prisons, but they hold imprisoned children.

I look up at the same time as the judge to see Fee Lo bringing a sleepy-eyed William Catherton Bennett into the courtroom. I almost feel sorry for Bennett—clearly he was the last to know about the hearing. It's no wonder no one called to let him know, because he doesn't exactly have any fans among his coworkers.

My pity for Bennett lasts only until I recall the way he pounced on me earlier that day, demanding that I agree for Phoebe to be "certified" as an adult tonight. Just because William Catherton Bennett and Phoebe's mother want Phoebe to be tried in a real courtroom for real murder chargers, doesn't mean that I'll ever agree to that.

I have a little surprise waiting for when Bennett tries to force my client into a plea. I've got a little theory building about Phoebe's drug-dealing, former football champ boyfriend. And unlike Phoebe, "Ace" is already an adult.

Bennet gives me his best Harvard sneer, and I frown back with narrowed eyes to let him know South Texas never runs from a fight.

But more importantly, this kid is still a kid. She still looks like a kid. But if Tuttle is as involved with all of this as I think he is, then this case may be a lot more complicated than it seems. It's clear from Phoebe's current state that she's no stranger to drugs, and clearly Tuttle has been in a position to exercise control over her for the last three years at least. I wouldn't be surprised if my investigation also revealed that Phoebe was a victim of sexual abuse or even trafficking. While never convicted of anything that could send him to prison for longer than short stretches, I know Tuttle will have an impressive record if I can get my hands on it. If I remember right, Tuttle was even involved with the smear campaign that led to the early retirement of the judge sitting before us now.

Bennett gives me short shrift as he slides into his chair, looking like he might nod off again. The judge, who has been waiting, calls the case.

We both stand.

I help Phoebe stand with the help of the deputy, and we prepare for the judge's questions.

CHAPTER TWO:
Arraignment

"You're being arraigned," I tell Phoebe. She looks more or less lucid, although I am relatively certain that she is still floating in space somewhere, the drugs leaving her system not letting her come back down to Earth yet. The cooperative and alert act might be for the judge's benefit, however. She is aware enough to remember her skills about controlling her world.

"I'm scared," she says and seems calmer when she looks at me again and leans into me from her place between me and the deputy, who dressed her. But then, I guess to put me in my place, she shoves me away from her with kitten-weak arms.

Evie, who has seen the entire thing, exclaims: "That's wild. Drug-induced anger probably. Sometimes, it hits kids that way coming off them. Son-of-a-bitch who sells it to them needs to be found and put away for a long time."

"He will be," I say. "He was there in the room with her when it happened; but he skipped."

With a grip on Phoebe's arm, I turn her my way and whisper, stressing each syllable: "The Judge is going to tell you how much trouble you are in. I don't have a clue as to where this will ultimately end up. So, let's hear what he says and don't say anything so you can help me defend you. Please don't say anything that is not a direct answer to his questions. It is definitely going to be some level of murder," I tell her. "And I need you to listen closely because in the worst case, this could result in life in jail."

I let her go, but reach out to stroke her hair again. That was the only thing that she had a positive response to earlier. She looks pitifully scared and alone, even standing between Evie and me. I shift a bit so her shoulder is resting against mine. I spot a small smile on her face as she leans into my shoulder a bit.

Truthfully, right this minute, I still don't want this case. I never mind having Fee Lo get me up for PC hearings. They aren't usually too difficult for me, since probable cause hearings just test the strength of the state's case and the evidence against my client. I don't sleep well anyway, and I'm always willing to give the case to another lawyer after the requirement of having an arraignment hearing within 48 hours is met. While sometimes these middle of the night arraignments are just overseen by a magistrate, it's no surprise that Fee Lo managed to get a judge to appear for Phoebe's hearing.

I can feel Phoebe shaking, and I wonder if it is from fear or just from the stress her body has endured over the past day. She's a confusing one for sure, responding to a gentle hand and then lashing out again. In spite of the shove a moment ago, I hope she really will accept my help in getting her through this mess she's in.

The judge shuffles his papers. He probably is waiting for the State (still nodding in his chair) to make a move. Bennet must have had very few all-nighters—a time when I did my best work—in college, if he becomes this much of a zombie from losing part of a single night's sleep.

It's possible that the judge is waiting for someone else. Phoebe keeps looking over her shoulder every few minutes as if she is expecting someone. Her grandfather, I assume. Then again, maybe this retired senior district judge never counted on being in a concrete block hole-in-the-wall courtroom like this.

He probably had to drive a ways to get here, since the Detention Center is halfway between Galveston and Texas City. The only nice-looking thing about it is the oil refinery visible from the parking lot, glowing poisonous and fiery across the dark water.

I never counted on being here either, but I've come to appreciate the work I do at the Center. I consider it a good life most of the time, and more importantly, it's a life I live on my own terms. As a lawyer, I learn something every day, and sometimes even get to make a positive difference for someone. I depend on appointments from judges like Baker for clients who can't afford to hire a lawyer. Sometimes the work is hard and emotional. But working here has shown me the extent of my own abilities. Some days, I am good at my job. And other days, I am fabulous.

I remain standing, a courtesy to the judge that is drilled in our heads in law school. A lawyer should never sit when addressing the court, but apparently Bennett missed that lecture. The judge may be causing a purposeful delay. He also may simply be adjusting to a courtroom in which his bench is a library table taken out of storage and placed on a painted plywood riser. He does seem to have a decent chair up there, and two flags frame the makeshift bench to mimic the atmosphere of a proper courtroom. The accommodations definitely suggest salvage, maybe a cleaning out of the county warehouse. Behind me a covey of regular straight chairs, also of the library variety, provide seats for visitors.

I pull up the complaint on the computer provided for counsel at my table and wait out the Judge. Finally, he decides to call the docket. Evie and I nudge Phoebe to stand up straight and face him.

Bennett reluctantly stands back up. I know Bennett's a Harvard graduate who was praised for his decision to come to this county and work as an assistant district attorney. He's currently running against the very DA who got him his job. Most of us who know him in a professional capacity know that he's not ready for the big time, but he seems oblivious to all his own shortcomings. Other lawyers say he is wet behind the ears. Even I, who could be called equally wet, can see how unqualified he is for the position he currently holds, much less for DA. He doesn't play well with others, and though he and I have been practicing for the same period of time, I suspect that I have more practical experience.

As the judge prepares to question Phoebe to acquire the routine jurisdictional information, Bennett leans on his table, looking like he's barely paying attention.

"What is your name, Miss?" the judge asks.

"Phoebe Sunshine MacPearson."

"Date of birth?"

"April 30, 2012."

"Are you sixteen years old?"

"Yes sir, sixteen or twenty-two."

I interrupt before she explains that she uses two ages and false ids. "She's sixteen, Your Honor."

"Thank you, Counsel. Are your parents present?"

"Poppi's coming," she says.

"Why don't you all be seated," the Judge says and begins his instructions. He speaks in a surprisingly scholarly voice as he begins. "Every person who is accused of a crime..." *The man sounds like a Judge ought to, I think.* ". . .has a right to remain silent, the right to have an attorney present when questioned by the government, and the right to have an attorney appointed if he cannot afford to hire a lawyer. These things are Constitutional requirements set out by the United States Supreme Court in the *Miranda* case in 1966."

Phoebe seems as lulled by the soft-spoken power of his speech as I am.

"The things you say during an arraignment hearing can be used against you in the trial of your case," he explains to Phoebe. He is talking with her like she's a child rather than making a formal pronouncement.

She seems to be listening.

As a practical matter, I know what she says will not be used against her after this hearing. There's no reporter present to make a record: the state's attorney seems oblivious to the fact that it is his duty to ask for one. I don't want one, necessarily, because generally anything my clients own up to is not in their best interest to have on any record.

I don't know where this judge did his training. He sounds patrician, out of place in this makeshift courtroom, but he also appears to be making the best of it. That voice of his reaches in and touches my soul. I finally place it: he is as winning as Roosevelt was to folks during his "Fireside Chats" during the Great Depression and World War II. He brought them comfort. I remember in my first psychology class, the professor said that Roosevelt was successful because he said what the nation wanted to hear and he said it in words they understood. The nation loved him because they related to him. He lifted all to his level. My favorite great-aunt remembered touching the radio during those talks because it made her feel connected to the President.

Bennett finally awakens enough to make his motion to certify. "The juvenile opposes the motion, Your Honor."

I know that this judge and most other judges in Texas will not certify a child that fast, but I am ready to oppose it if Judge Baker takes Bennett's motion for Phoebe to be certified as an adult seriously. The Judge has to screen everything about the Juvenile before making that determination. Most judges hardly ever certify anyway—we have Juvenile Courts for that very purpose.

"The issue for counsel is the conduct, Your Honor," I say. "But the first consideration must be the child. She is clearly not advanced, and was also under the effect of drugs supplied to her by a nefarious adult, who may, in fact, be found also to be a responsible party for these charges."

"That's ridiculous. Your Honor, she can't possibly have proof of that at this point."

"Thank you, Counsel," the judge says. He begins reading the charges.

"Your Honor, if I may," I interrupt. "We waive the reading of the full complaint." I let Phoebe slide into her chair.

"We waive the full reading of the charges and would appreciate a little more time to locate the parents or grandparent and get them here so she can be treated appropriately. Miss MacPearson enters a plea of "not true."

"Huh?" she says, interrupting. "I did it!" she insists. "And she had it coming!"

"Counsel," he says, looking at me. "I agree with you; she does not have the capacity to help you, at this time. I am going to recess this hearing until 1 p.m. this afternoon. Maybe things will look a little better for your juvenile then."

Bennett slams his file against his table and storms out of the courtroom, not seeking permission or moving for leave to do so. Evie takes Phoebe by the arm again to lead her out of the room as well.

"Asshole," Phoebe Sunshine MacPearson calls out; but it is to the judge and not the angry prosecutor that she speaks. She continues to call out as they lead her back to her cell, throwing the specific threat: "You will get yours, motherfucker!"

Her tiny little voice is cut off finally by the closing of the door that shuts with its wretched moan of metal striking metal.

CHAPTER THREE:
The Judge

"Your Honor, I apologize for my client. She is still under the effect of the drugs, I think."

"That's okay, Counsel," I say to the young lawyer, McLeod. "I agree with you. She lacks capacity at this time to assist you: I suspect from lingering effects of the drugs. We'll see how things are this afternoon."

As I gather up my papers and prepare to leave, I consider my evening, if it can still be called that. I'll go home and get what sleep I can, then be right back in this so-called courtroom for the afternoon docket.

While this isn't my first introduction to juvenile law, it's certainly an interesting one. Lilly Pruser asked me to sit for her this week so that she could go to Missouri to visit her mother who is ill. Lilly warned me it was possible I might be called out at night, but I had no warning that it would be like this.

First the commissioner called at midnight. "Judd, I won't talk about the case," Bull MacPearson said. It was the way most of these forced *ex parte* conversations started. Most lawyers know and respect that they cannot talk to the judge one-on-one unless the other side is present.

"Bull," I acknowledged. "I don't think we *can* even talk if she's got a case."

"Yeah, I know, I know, Judd. But I think Phoebe Sunshine's got herself in a little bit of trouble again—different trouble from the usual. Probably still over that peckerwood Ace Tuttle, but this time's different."

"I really need to hang up, Bull," I said. "You have to call the lawyers first."

"I know it, Judd, but it's Phoebe.

"Goodbye, Bull."

With Lilly out of town and Tamara off for the weekend, it fell to me to fill in.

"The prosecutor's running for promotion," Deputy Hernandez told me. "He's already talking certification as an adult, Judge, and saying no question exists about guilt or innocence. He wants to take it across town tonight and recharge her there as an adult. Thirty kids witnessed it, but the report says they were all drunk. He says the mom has joined in on his motion so her child will have justice in a real courthouse. She refuses to come to the Center. Judge, I can't let this prosecutor take over this process."

"Thank you, deputy, I'm coming out there. It might be an hour depending on how quick I can get out the door."

I knew it was inevitable that I'd need to make a middle-of-the-night appearance as soon as the deputy called. I got out of bed, pulled on trousers, left my old t-shirt on, passed a washcloth over my face, and headed out the door.

Hardly the most put-together I'd ever been for court, but it was a juvenile case. At the time, I didn't know what a mess this case would end up being. As I continue to sort through my papers, I look up to see Betsy, doing something with the computer on the bench.

"Do you know whether Hernandez did PC and ordered tests?" I ask Betsy.

"I'll check, Judge. I don't really know."

"Did you call Judge Pruser?"

"I don't think he's talked to her. We've been trying to get a hold of her ever since we got notice of this case. Fee Lo says she's probably on the road, but I don't think she's going to be back that quickly. She has two more days off, so you may need to cover for her."

"Maybe she'd be willing to come back sooner."

"Her phone's off, Judge," Hernandez says, joining the conversation. "She's traveling. Driving at night so the kids will sleep."

I shake my head, knowing he is right. I know Lilly well: she prefers driving all night to managing fighting kids all day.

"You might not want to take this case, Judge. It's going to be a rough one." Hernandez says, giving me an out.

"Might not be my choice," I say. "But I drew it fair and square. I won't back out now. At least, until Lilly gets back."

The deputy chuckles. "If it was me, I wouldn't touch it with a ten-foot pole."

"It's hardly a choice though, really. Given the circumstances, I agree that a judge should hear it, and I'm here. Suppose I'll see you at one?"

"It would help if you beat the press here. Docket's at one so they'll be swarming in by noon."

I nod at Hernandez, who steps away to finish up. Looking down at the papers in hand, I compare the description of the juvenile from the sheriff's report—quiet, unresisting, likely high—to what I saw of Phoebe Sunshine MacPearson tonight. I can still hear the girl shouting something no doubt rude from beyond the doors of the courtroom.

Bull said '*real different.*' Understatement of the year.

I continue ignoring the girl so I won't have to hold her in contempt for the shouts and threats. She hardly looks big enough to carry out any threat, but she does have that determined look about her. Even if I wasn't familiar with her family, one look at her would tell me that she's one of those kids that receive more money than parenting. Usually, when I sit for Lilly or Tamara, I see poor, underprivileged kids. Tonight, it is the monied child who, in the face of trouble, is standing alone. She may very well have put herself in this position, but it's still sad to see.

I look at the name on the order I have just signed and motion toward Alexandra McLeod, who is standing there but somehow not looking as disarrayed as I'm sure I do on such short notice. Even at nearly 3:30 A.M. in casual clothes, she's attractive. And she seems to know her stuff.

"I signed your order," I say. "I'll ask Hernandez to make you a copy."

"He's busy trying to get the mother's attention. I'll do it, Judge." Evie interrupts, approaching the bench to take the order. "I'll give it to the clerks when they get here."

At least the attorney has the good sense not to argue. I'd like to tell her I won't remember the child's confession if anyone asks me, but most would know I can't testify in a case I'm trying anyway. One advantage of being old is you can decide what you hear and what you don't hear most of the time.

I nod a goodbye to the young lawyer, wondering briefly if she really did somehow beat me here, or if she was already on the premises to visit Hernandez. Lilly loves to talk my ear off about her workplace gossip, which often centers around the women who fall all over that little Latino. He is good-looking, I decide. But she's cute too.

Papers in order, I pick up my briefcase.

"You can leave that if you like, Judge," Hernandez calls out. "I can lock it in the Judge's Chamber 'til you get back."

"Thank you, deputy; that's a good deal."

CHAPTER FOUR:
The Judge and the Encounter

The clock on the dash shows three-forty-five in the morning. Judd stifles a second yawn. He's had no sleep for nearly 24 hours.

He was reading when Bull and then Deputy Hernandez called. This assignment has left him feeling even more fearful about the state of the youth. The world has seemed more out of whack than ever since the Pandemic.

He turns his vehicle onto the blacktop that will take him away from the Detention Center for Juveniles. He has at least a good forty-five minutes to go before being able to settle in for the night.

The road is empty; but lights reach up as tall as trees to line the shore from the oil refineries that stay up and running all night. It seems festive in the early morning quiet.

A larger vehicle cuts into the silence, pulling out from a side road and racing toward him, flicking its lights to bright. Shocked, he watches it speed in his direction, wondering if another problem has hit the Center. He glances down—his cell phone is quiet, the screen not lighted, as it would be if they were trying to call him. He slows, moving to the right to let the larger vehicle pass. But the truck slows too and rides his bumper, looming tall in the rearview mirror. He waits for a signal to pull over, but none comes.

The truck whips out to come around him, cutting faster than it should on this narrow black strip of asphalt so close to the sea at tide. The truck is going so fast the driver loses control. The truck swerves off to the left in the wrong direction and before the driver can get control, it knocks down the sign that points toward the Center's entrance. A high spray splashes from the salty remainder as the truck plows through water on its side of the road and bumps itself back onto the roadbed.

Judd slows and pulls as far to the right as he can. The swampy bar ditch along the highway keeps him from pulling off the road altogether. The water comes right up to the edge of the asphalt like the ends of the earth, smooth and glossy in the moonlight. The Bay can't quite conquer this strip of pavement. The truck straightens out and comes in his direction once more—this time aimed for the driver's side of the car.

He pulls back onto the road to try to pull forward and away, but the banged up old truck swerves again to pull alongside his little Prius. The truck's passenger-side window is down and the driver is calling out something. Judd can't hear the words over the noise of the road, but can't mistake the angry tone being yelled in his direction.

Finally, it sinks in. The girl's warning: "You'll get yours!"

This driver is aiming a gun at him! Even in the early morning darkness, the driver's eyes burn in the reflected light off the dash.

A contemptuous look on a young face. Chin jutting out. Hair standing on end. Eyes boring intently in his direction.

He knows that face. This young man was waiting for the girl. Still obsessed.

This guy sure needs help, Judd thinks.

The truck again whips off the road. It plows a trench alongside the berm and comes back up behind his car, playing a deadly game now of cat and mouse between the gigantic truck and the small car. Head beams flip back to high as the beat-up old truck moves in behind him and again bears down on the bumper, blinding Judd in the rearview mirror. He tries using the side mirrors to look around the truck, but visibility is no better on either side. He virtually loses sight of the actual truck in the intense whiteness of its bright headlights.

The world takes on an eerie, surreal feeling. Judd feels disassembled, no footing left on Earth. Gravity has lost its pull. His small steel and aluminum box bounces as it goes over the lip of the asphalt. He can feel the resistance as he forces it back onto the black strip. The berm, holding back the sea, is right there.

This man has something to do with her.

Not her.

The other one. She came to help.

Out in the middle of the night to take care of one crazy kid, his life is being threatened by another. He should have just stayed at the Center like that lawyer, slept on Lilly's couch.

The truck bounces against the car, trying to push it off the road and into the ditch by the berm, but Judd holds tightly to the wheel.

It makes contact again, and sticks this time with a metallic screech. He can feel the car moving sideways, tight grip on the wheel doing nothing.

The high beams from the truck veer to the side as the two vehicles move together, pointing toward a dark sky lit by few stars.

Refineries in the distance glow like Christmas.

Despite the pollution, Judd always liked this horizon at night. The quiet lapping of the water under the artificial starlight.

His mouth dry and heart pounding like it hasn't since his Navy days, he tries again to yank the wheel away from the ditch. The car hardly moves at all, the pair of vehicles locked in a sick dance.

He can see with clarity now the gun extended from a long-fingered hand through the truck's window. It fires, shattering the glass between them. The man fires again, leaving a mosquito bite just off his ear on the left side.

The truck yanks itself away from the smaller car with a lurch. For a moment Judd thinks he's in the clear, until the car, independent of his grip on the wheel, starts to roll. Everything blurs into impact and noise.

The car rolls.

And again.

It rocks sideways, left to right.

Then it slows.

Then it stops.

The engine makes no sound in the inverted car.

The car is lodged in the ditch that runs along the berm to hold back the water from the Bay at high tide. Murky brown water pours into the open gap of the window where the bullet shattered the glass. The ceiling of the car soon swims with muddy water, lapping around Judd's face. A small pinpoint on his skull seeps a dark substance into the steadily-rising water.

Judd is aware of a dull pain below his ear, and a sharp pain where the seatbelt is digging into his shoulder where he hangs upside down. Then, as the adrenaline subsides and the water rises, he becomes aware of nothing at all.

All fear is gone as the blackness encloses itself around him and brings quiet. As his heart rate slows, the only rhythm left is the regular lapping of the water.

CHAPTER FIVE:
The Reporter

As a reporter, there are times when you have to choose between the story right in front of you, and going after a better story elsewhere. Inside the Detention Center is a sure story: local girl pops a cap in her best friend's face, is too high to flee the scene. But this reporter's instincts tell him an even better story is driving away from the Center right now in a familiar little car. Mickey Little decides to follow the judge. He should have stayed retired, after all the work Little did to force him out.

He can practically smell the coming story as he watches an oversized truck pull out behind the judge, trailing close behind. Little's been in the news business so long, he never doubts that sense when it comes over him. He's worked so many cities in Texas that he can pretty much tell you where all the bodies are buried. Knows half the government workers in the counties he's worked. Most of the elected officials he's challenged over the years are waiting for the day they can piss on his grave.

But Mickey Little doesn't care. He sees himself as an old-school crusader. His blood runs blacker than printer's ink. The more pissers he can add to the list before he dies, the better.

He follows the truck and judge's car, careful to not get too close. It wouldn't do to spook them and ruin whatever scene is being laid out. The beat up pick up was there when Little pulled into the Center's parking lot earlier, but he didn't pay it much attention. Getting a better look at it now, he can see that it's jacked up on oversized tires, with spiky Medieval-looking hubcaps that cannot be street legal.

Wonder what kind of driver would drive a mess like that?

The truck waits a few minutes, until the caravan of the three of them are a few miles away from the Detention Center. The old truck races right up to the rear of the Prius and hugs the judge's bumper. The truck blasts its high beams into the rear of the car.

Little pulls out his compact Olympus, bracing it with one hand on the dash as he speeds up to get closer to the scene, clicking the camera as fast as it will shoot. As he pulls close, the truck swings out again into the lane to pass just as he gets close enough to read the license plate: TLC-something. *That will be easy to remember.*

What he sees next is Pulitzer material.

He clicks away as the truck swerves back to bump the little car. The Prius leaves the road, wobbles, and overturns, rolling up against the berm. It rolls again before coming to a stop, settling into the ditch filled with muddy water.

The truck burns rubber for about a hundred yards before the driver gets it under control and disappears into the night. Little pulls his car off the road and, camera in hand, runs to the overturned car to start recording the scene.

The judge's head is about half-buried in muddy water. Deciding the story is now photographs of a dead judge, hanging upside down by his seat belt, he starts clicking away like any reporter would. Instinct tells him he should do something heroic but he can only stand there, clicking away at the dead judge.

Habit can't be overturned.

He steps back from the car. Takes more photos. He comes to his senses long enough to search his pockets until he finds his cell phone and hits 911, giving location and emergency. "It's too late to be much good. He's upside down by his seat belt and he's in the water. No way is he breathing."

Again, click, click. Step to the side. More photos. A sudden brain-wave has him calling the Center to let them know they have a dead judge.

He steps up to the car, giving it a shove. It rocks a bit, stirring the water, but doesn't move. He pushes again, with the same result. The water surges, either with the tide or from the car moving, but the judge's head remains in the water.

He's starting to lose the feel of this story. His never-wrong in-stincts are telling him that he may have messed this one up.

Within minutes of the call, the deputy from the Center arrives. He parks in the road, leaving his flashing overhead lights on but the siren off, pulls out the knife in his waist kit, and kneels in the muddy water to grab the judge. Lifting his head above water, he cuts the seatbelt.

The judge's body levels out, the lower half moving into the water, the upper held out of the water by the deputy, now up to his own chest.

"Got ya'self locked in," Little observes. The deputy is pinned inside the car in order to hold the judge's head above water.

"Get back, Little," the deputy orders. "Stay out of my emergency zone, I've got somebody here who's in trouble."

"Probably dead at this point. And I'm staying right here. Don't forget freedom of the press."

"There's no freedom to endanger someone. Move *back*! That's an order."

"I can help you with this one," he says, leaning into the car to get a better angle. The intermittent camera flashes light up the judge's face so he can see the wound. It's still ebbing a thick substance that looks like coagulating blood. He watches the deputy try to slide the judge, moving him as little as possible. He gets one hand on the judge's neck, then smiles.

The judge is still alive.

Very interesting.

The real story is the source of the gunshot wound—the driver of a vehicle with a license plate beginning with TLC. No tender loving care for the judge, that's for sure.

The deputy continues to slide carefully, his own body providing support for the judge's.

"I saw the truck that did this to him. I got pictures and I got part of the license plate. Old dirty messed up piece of junk on wheels big enough for an earthmover. License tag TLC."

"I gotcha," the deputy says. "But if you shine that flash one more time into this car, I am going to arrest you for interfering with police activity. Under the circumstances, it might even be a felony because you know and understand that you're impeding my ability to rescue this man. Stand back, damn you. I need to get him out and get him breathing again!"

He steps back, raising both hands in mock surrender. "Ok, dickless,

I hear you. I give up. You interfere with the First Amendment all you want: you know I'll get the last word."

With that, he crosses to his vehicle and sits sideways in the doorway to ruminate on how this story will read. He's added one more dickless prick to the line at Little family plot and he couldn't be prouder. As many as want to can add their drips to his resting place. The more public figures Little pisses off, the better he figures he's doing his job. Public figures, defined in his favorite Supreme Court case, *Sullivan v. The New York Times*, mostly have no rights to privacy. His goal is to put every one of those dickless bastards on page one.

They like to call him dickless. A cruel nickname that he wears like a badge of honor. He's not afraid to call attention to it: Public pricks have little dicks!

"How you doin', dickless," Little says to high and low. It gets them going. "See you on page one, dickless," just to put the fear of God in their heads for a day or two. Only he can wage his wars on page one.

Little knew before leaving home this morning that the little dick commissioner had called the little dick judge. He had assumed that the granddaughter's release was fixed: the commissioner would demand she be allowed to leave under his guidance. She would stroll on out of there smiling on her grandfather's arm, just like the last time she messed up and ended up in the Center. No MacPearson would spend a night in jail.

Probable cause is whatever the judge who makes the ruling says it is, and he's seen some big ones slide through. Even with a murder charge on the table, as his confidential informer informed him that evening, if Bull MacPearson wanted a finding of *no PC*, it was certain he would get it, whoever the judge happens to be.

Little staked out the entrance of the Center to get his photo of the commissioner and his granddaughter leaving together. But none of that panned out as he had foreseen. Something went wrong. Really wrong.

MacPearson never showed. No other family member showed. The girl went back into lock-up, spewing threats against the judge and everybody.

"You'll get yours," his contact said the girl shouted at the judge. And it looks like he did!

A siren sounds in the distance, coming closer. The blinking lights are about a mile away, blending with the lights from the refinery. The deputy is still huffing and puffing, having slid the judge onto the pavement and laid him out flat. The deputy keeps busy giving CPR until the ambulance finally pulls up and the EMTs take over. Again, Little needs to decide whether to stay for the story in front of him, or follow the ambulance for the story there. He decides to stay, but also calls his opposition at Channel 13 with a half-correct anonymous lead on the story. No one's stealing Mickey Little's thunder, not tonight.

CHAPTER SIX:
The Brain

You can't tell everything that's going on here and I know that my man looks dead to a non-thinking brain from the outside, which that reporter is.

Non-thinking.

For all practical purposes, my man could be viewed as dead, but I am as busy inside here as a check-out clerk at Walmart with a long line.

I'm trying to ward off disaster, checking and by-passing systems like crazy!

You-son-of-a-you-know-what!

Get that flash out of my man's face!

Move back! You're taking up my man's air.

Does he move?

I mutter to myself: of course not! He doesn't move.

This numb nut is an animal. Not all reporters are but he is.

An animal. And scum. He has no class.

Get your filthy hands off my man's head!

Can't you see that blood?

Get away!

Does he move? I mutter to myself, but he won't move.

What about those pictures? Do I have to let him get away with that? I shake things so they'll be fuzzy.

It's so dark in here and wet!

Oh, Holy Christ, please don't let it end this way. We still have things we need to do in life. Good things for you!

It's up to you, Buddy, I tell my man. Understand that it is up to you for this to happen. You can't give up now. No slacking either.

Keep it going.

Give me a little help here, Buddy.

Breathe for me!

The deputy arrives and cuts the seatbelt off.

Bless you, Deputy!

Takes his head out of water.

Bless you, Deputy!

Keeping his head from the water, he lets his body settle onto the inside roof of the car.

Is he breathing on his own? I ask about my man.

"Come on judge, you can do it!" the deputy says to him.

"uh one,"

"uh two,"

"uh three,"

That's My Man!

Thank God, I hear that siren.

Is that light coming around the corner?

That's it, My Man. You're doing it.

"And uh nine and uh ten and uh"

. . . Here we go!

"What the fuh...?"

Are you back again?

Ah, relief. At last.

That's it, Deputy, pull him out far enough for them to grab him.

Slowly goes it.

That wound's still draining.

Seeping, not pulsing, that's good.

Attaboy, My Man,

You did it, Son! You and that deputy!

What the hell? Get out of here, flash machine.

That's all you are good for!

Listen to the deputy! Numb nut. Get that effing light out of the way.

Can't you tell an emergency when you're in it?

Don't breathe your fetid dog breath on my man!

You've made me lose my composure!

CHAPTER SEVEN:
The Deputy

Can this night get any worse?" Felipe asks his dispatcher, who is already calling for Life Flight and state troopers to assist.

"Don't leave," he tells Shadow. "We might need you." He opens the Judge's Chambers and tells her that she is free to sleep on the judge's couch and to help Evie process anybody brought in while he is gone.

"Lock down!" he orders, buckling on his utility belt and putting on his vest.

Felipe runs to his car and is out of the parking lot before the dispatcher finishes directions to the others. He knows which way to go. There is only one way home for the Judge to take. Calling for back-up, he reaches the scene, stops his car across half of the road to create a roadblock and shuts down the siren, leaving the overheads flashing.

His stomach turns when the judge's Prius comes into focus. Judd Baker's car sits upside down and the judge's head is half buried in the murky water that is pooled at the edge of the asphalt road.

Felipe runs to the car, taking his knife from his waist kit on the way. He cuts the seatbelt and lets the judge's body sink into his arms, which dig into the mud before he can get enough of a grip on the judge's shoulders to keep his head above water. They both sink into the muddy mess in the small interior of the car. The bottom half of Baker's limp body sinks into the rounded roof of the car as the deputy places a finger on the judge's neck and welcomes a faint, irregular beating.

"He's a goner," a voice that Felipe Hernandez could best describe as weathered comes at him from over his shoulder.

"Not yet," Hernandez says as the reporter flashes away with his camera. "If you don't mind," he says, motioning the reporter away. "Move away."

"Remember, freedom of the press," the reporter barks.

"Have a little decency then," Hernandez says, turning his body as much as he can to block the camera's view of the judge. Another flash of light fills the interior of the car.

Felipe sees the wound on the side of the judge's head.

Hearing the siren over his shoulder, Felipe knows the EMTs are less than a mile away and will be here within a minute. He decides to deal with Dickless Little after he takes care of the judge. The bleeding wound on the side of the judge's head appears to be coagulating. Felipe straightens his own position and tries to straighten out the judge's airway without moving him so much that it sets off faster bleeding. They move an inch at a time, using Felipe's body on the ground as a foundation for holding the judge's body as straight as he can manage. Stacked that way, he inches the judge's body through the window space, despite the shattered glass pieces that try to catch on his uniform.

Without offering any help while Felipe crawls out of the car bearing the judge's weight, the reporter now leans in close again to tell him: "I saw the truck that did this to him. I got pictures and I got part of the license plate. Old dirty messed up piece of junk on wheels big enough for an earthmover. License tag TLC."

Felipe glares at the reporter as best he can through the flashes of the camera. Mickey Little, who everyone calls Dickless, has always been a piece of work, but this is on another level. "If you shine that flash one more time into this car, I am going to arrest you for interfering with police activity."

When the reporter responds with another flash, Felipe loses his temper a bit. "Stand back, damn you. I need to get him out and get him breathing again. Step back unless you want me to put you in my backseat once I get the judge out of here."

"You won't," Dickless says. "You *threatening* the press?" The reporter then adds as if an afterthought: "Pedro?"

The deputy ignores the taunt; Mickey Little knows Hernandez' name but has an extremely irritating habit of calling every Hispanic officer he sees *Pedro* or *Jesús*.

Felipe decides to bide his time until the EMTs take care of the judge and get him to Life Flight, knowing that he will confiscate that camera before Dickless Little gets away from the scene.

CHAPTER EIGHT:
The Brain Returns

Permit me to introduce myself. I am a bit calmer now!

We are in the ambulance, heading for a rendezvous with the helicopter, which would have been my choice from the beginning.

But the EMTs on the ambulance actually get my seal of approval.

They recognized time was of the essence and they already have us aboard at the first place Life Flight could land, a parking lot about a half mile away from the Center. They have my man on oxygen already and they are working his vitals as we fly. They can do everything but major surgery on this beauty of the air.

We are going to Sealy, which is my choice as well. I trust a hospital that continues its mission where it started rather than sneaking across the Bay the way others have done since the first sign of trouble after that last Hurricane, which was our worst one in twenty years.

Now that we have a brief hiatus from the chaos, I can properly introduce myself to you and tell you who I am and why you have to trust me for a time for the story.

I am the brain of the man seriously wounded here.

I do not say fatally wounded because I am determined that we are not going out this way! I have a lot of reserve to draw on because my man is in good health for his age.

But, in fact, I am the 75 percent of his brain that he knows nothing about.

Your circumstances are the same; so please don't be threatened. Know that you actually need me and if you do have an accident at some point, it is I who will come first to your rescue and keep things going while others treat the broken parts.

So trust me.

You actually want me here.

Just like they say about the Marines when they come in.

I do the things every day that you don't want to spend time thinking about or maybe you are so busy, that you don't have the luxury of doing for yourself.

I breathe for you.

I walk, sleep, eat, and digest for you.

I keep your blood pressure up, and I keep your heart rate down.

I do it all.

You just don't know me.

That is the way it is for everyone. I live within you like a big parasite that has control over everything. But we are symbiotic.

The writer said I am your Mission Control!

You are four pounds at most, you say, as if that makes a difference. But my four pounds makes more magic than the stars in the milky way and we do it right here inside your head.

Go with the flow; you'll find that I am right!

Not that my man listens to my better judgment.

And you probably don't listen to your higher brain either. If we did, we would not keep getting into these scrapes.

Uh-oh, we are beginning to spiral down toward that circle!

Wow! That can lift your stomach right up into your throat!

"Hang on Judd! We've got you, Sir!" a medic calls out as he opens the door and lets a nurse push us out toward him.

"Here take this line and hold it up so we can keep the juice flowing," the Life Flight nurse tells her companion, who jumps out as he runs beneath the still turning rotors; and although the power is cut and the props are settling, he seems to know exactly how much to bend down.

I open my folders to get Judd ready for this.

I can't let him sleep!

We have to be awake and at our best for this phase.

CHAPTER NINE:
The Granddaughter

"As soon as Phoebe got back to her cell," Evie tells me, "She shucked off the coveralls and threw them across the cell."

"I guess our era of understanding is over." I say.

"This is probably just a hissy fit. Less to do with the drugs and more to do with being a spoiled brat."

I smile because I am sure she's right on.

"You need to put this on, Phoebe," I tell my client. She's sitting there like she's in shock because Poppi didn't show up and she's not going home. Reality is cascading in.

There is a physical side to it she can't help. She is not able to control the shaking that wracks her body. She had to remain in the cell as ordered, but she chose not to wear the scratchy clothes that she tolerated to see the judge. At 103 pounds, she's skin and bones, but it's her own fault if she refuses to wear the covering provided.

"That makes it worse, sweetheart," I say, trying for persuasion. "And the clothes they gave you might not be designer, but they're clean and will keep you warm."

"They don't feel clean to me, Shadow," she says.

"Miss Evie says they come straight from the laundry."

"But they're not ironed and they're scratchy," she insists.

"Here," I tell her. "Take my sweater. It's pretty old and broken in, but it's soft and definitely not scratchy." I say this with a smile and a careful caress over her messy hair. Like magic, she again calms down.

She sticks her arms into the sleeves and, as I thought it would, the sweater covers her like a long coat. As if to avoid something else, like saying thank you, she carefully studies her manicured nails with their chipped stars and stripes where her hands peep from the sweater's arms. She does not take it off but draws it even tighter around her.

"I can do this," she tells me. "When they give me back my real clothes, I will dress." She crosses her legs on the single bed on which she half lies and half sits, and tries closing her eyes tightly, but they flash open. I sense the problem: if she can't see the women, they don't matter, but what she sees when she closes her eyes is probably worse.

She struggles to keep her eyes open, trying not to even blink. Tears run down her face and drop onto my sweater in big splashes. I hug her shoulders because there is nothing and nobody else to do it.

Apparently, the scene playing in her head will not go away.

Having read her file, I know now that this girl has been in and out of trouble most of her life. Now, it appears that she is finally beginning to understand that she has gotten herself into her biggest jam yet. Although her parting words to the judge were full of pure bravado, she must know this is different from the kind of trouble she's been in before. She actually admitted to me that she is scared— the first break-through since I set foot in the Center tonight.

Phoebe MacPearson has worked the system before, letting her Poppi call the shots and be there whenever she needed. Now, with her mother being so antagonistic, he may be all the family support she has. And since I talked to him, she doesn't even have that in the way she wants.

I'm going to avoid telling Phoebe this, but her grandfather listened to me when I urged him to stop just throwing money at the problem. He needs to recognize what is really happening with his granddaughter: she needs professional help.

I don't want to tell her this; but he authorized me to call in an expert to help us figure out both the problem and a solution. Altogether, he seemed like a man scared to death about all that he failed to see, but trying to make the most compassionate choice. He even agreed that she should not go home at this time.

No other soul from that family has made one visit to this Center since the child was brought in. Mom has her own feelings about where and how this child should be treated. She wants the State to throw the book at her because she no longer wants to have the trouble of dealing with her. Dad is on a social whirl of his own as a newly divorced man. And Grandpa is the standby parent, but he needs a refresher course for today's child.

Phoebe is essentially abandoned.

I also know from Evie that Hurley Brown, the family lawyer, told Phoebe that by morning he will have matters under control, and she will be headed home.

Along with her temporary lawyer, he says.

But he has a surprise coming. I don't intend to step aside now without a fight. This child needs a lawyer and not the enabler of the past who just might be protecting the real perpetrator in this case.

"I am going to take a nap before I have to get ready to go home," Phoebe says, while sucking in deep breaths. "I'll make sure I get your sweater back to you."

"You have to," I say. "It's my security blanket sweater; that's why I brought it here."

"You can leave now," she says but she smiles and hugs the sweater to her.

"I need to talk to you about something, Phoebe," I say. She rolls over on the cot, clutching the sweater around her. Looks up at me.

"If you are going to have me as your lawyer, I want to talk about what happened. There might be a solution I want us to start thinking about."

"The kids at the house said Tuttle gave you and your friend drugs to have you do *your stuff*. They said she was new and you were helping him train her. Is any of this familiar, Phoebe?"

She gives me a blank face.

"What does *stuff* mean, Phoebe?"

"Your guess is as good as mine," she says, looking cold stone sober at this point. "They're always saying some shit."

"Is Tuttle selling access to your body to other men? Is he getting you to bring in other girls from the school?"

"Not that I know about."

I know I need to try another tactic.

"Phoebe, if I am going to be your lawyer, you have to talk to me."

"Of course I am going to have you as my lawyer," she says. "I can't go through this without you."

"Then I want you to start thinking about going to a place where they can get you off the drugs and keep you safe from Tuttle. You can receive treatment for everything that's been happening to you."

"You find somewhere that'll take me and I'll do it," she says. "I really want to take a nap now before Hurley gets me out."

I can almost hear her saying: *Let these bitches see how little I care about what they are doing to me.*

But at least the sweater offers her a little bit of modesty.

And within twenty-four hours, I will learn just how easily my little client lies.

A few hours later, in the front office at the Center, the phone rings. All three of us lurch for it, but Evie wins.

"What do we know about the judge?" she asks first off. I assume it's Fee Lo, but it isn't. Sergeant Rogers with the DPS is reporting in. Evie puts him on speaker.

"Fee Lo will be a while," he says. "We have a bulletin out for little Henry Ace Tuttle and his black truck, which should have some major dents in it. Fee Lo says to watch out because he was apparently sitting out there waiting for the judge. We know Tuttle is armed because the judge has a bullet wound in his head."

I hear a soft *holy shit* from Evie.

"Fee Lo says Tuttle may be out there somewhere planning to come and get the girl." Rogers continues, "He says keep everything locked down tight: don't open the gate or the doors to him or anyone you don't know. We're giving help from the DPS since all Fee Lo has is Ismael Pope, who probably can't get here in time to be of any use. Fee Lo saved the judge's life and had him breathing when they finally got him on a Life Flight. He asked me to track the judge to Sealy so he could make sure they knew who he was and what happened. That's where I am now; the judge is in surgery."

I can't help it, a tear or two escapes at the thought of Baker in his current precarious state. I pretend I don't see Betsy and Evie swiping their eyes as well.

"I have two guys on their way to you as back-up. That reporter, Dickless, was apparently at the scene and saw the judge get shot and Tuttle flee. But Fee Lo says keep everything locked down: you know the judge's history with Dickless."

"So, about that back-up?" Evie asks.

"I'm sending a couple uniforms from DPS. Tatum and Stewart are coming from Texas City and Santa Fe. They'll be in marked cars and in uniform so don't let anybody else in."

"I know Stewart," Evie says. "He's been out here before. How old is Tatum?"

"Retirement," Rogers says.

"I'll probably recognize him then," Evie says. "Thanks for the help. Makes me feel better about our odds if Tuttle is planning to come around."

"It sure still don't look good," Rogers adds. "I would not let my guard down if I was you. But at least the judge has a chance now."

"Thank God," Betsy says.

"Either one of you girls got a gun?" Rogers asks.

"We women have our government-issued 9 mils," Evie says with a laugh, showing a little pride. "But I'd like some force on the outside here so he can't slip up on us."

"I hear ya," Rogers says. "I meant no insult."

"Didn't take any," she says, again smiling and taking him off speaker.

We don't hear the rest of it from our side. Evie finishes up the conversation and swears when she puts the phone down on her desk.

"That son-of-a-bitch Dickless," she exclaims. "Fee Lo is bringing him back here for the DPS to take him to the Galveston Jail. He's under protective arrest until Fee Lo can look at the pictures he claims caught the event. It might take him a while to check the pictures and process the scene since this is looking like an attempted homicide."

"That could take until tomorrow afternoon," Betsy says. "Fee Lo is the most meticulous investigator that I know. When he finishes checking the scene, there won't be nothing left to find. Remember the Comstock case?"

"Oh yes," Evie says, remembering a much-publicized murder in the neighborhood.

"I'm sure he won't finish until the sun comes up," I add.

"I think you're right. We need to divide up our time and try to get a short nap in before morning," Evie says. She is in charge. "You go first, Betsy, I'll need an armed deputy to take my place after the first shift. Shadow, it would help if you stay up with me until the sun comes up. I don't think Tuttle will try anything in daylight."

"I don't feel good trying to sleep with Tuttle out there," Betsy says. "I'll wait up with you until daylight."

"I will too," I say.

So the three of us sip coffee and settle in to wait for the sun.

CHAPTER TEN:
The Reporter

"The power of the press be damned," Deputy Felipe-fucking-Hernandez says after the judge has been taken away in the Life Flight helicopter, seizing Little's camera. "This camera contains evidence of a crime. It's my duty to secure the scene and everything in it, including what you said you saw. I have to see if the pictures corroborate with your claims."

Mickey knows that Hernandez has him by the short hairs.

"Even famous reporters like yourself can't withhold evidence of a crime. This could become a murder investigation for all we know." And Hernandez, that little nobody from the Valley, *smiles*. Mickey will testify to that.

"Maybe," Hernandez says and pauses. "You're my perpetrator. The whole world knows you led a smear campaign against this judge for years. It would be so easy to claim malice aforethought, with how much public hate you've thrown at Baker."

"My history with Baker has nothing to do with this," Mickey warns. "The driver of that truck did it. I got pictures! Great pictures of the crime in progress!"

"Then you've described yourself as the material witness," Hernandez adds. "And you weren't doing a thing to help the judge when I came on the scene. Until I see those pictures, it's as likely to me that you ran the judge off the road as saw it done. I would even say you were *gloating*, taking pictures of the poor judge without regard for his dire circumstances. You failed to even attempt to render aid; in fact, you got in the way. You and your camera."

"You can't take my camera," Little insists. "I'm a member of the

Fourth Estate and you have no jurisdiction to seize my notes!"

"I've already done it," Hernandez says. "It's not your notes. It's a camera on which you have related to me there is exculpatory evidence to show you didn't run the judge off the road and try to kill him. I'm taking you and the camera in."

"We'll see about that," Little warns. "You can't arrest me!"

"I am not leaving crucial evidence in the hands of a man who might be my perpetrator," Hernandez says. "Now, are we going to do this the easy way or not? Sit down, and stay there."

Mickey thinks he hears the cocky little shit mutter "*So much for bragging,*" as he walks away. "You damage that camera or those pictures and your sorry ass is dead," he calls out to Hernandez's back.

Little parks himself in the driver's seat of his car, legs hanging out the side and door swung into the roadway. He pulls out his cellphone again as the deputy takes his sweet time taking his own set of pictures of the scene.

To save his scoop, Little blocks his own number for anonymity and calls his number one opponent at Channel 13. He whispers into the phone, "Judge Judd Baker had a one car accident leaving the Detention Center in Galveston County this morning. No one knows how a judge who's sober could run off the road like that."

Still fuming, he calls his runner and tells him to give the same half-true tip to everyone else on his list. Hernandez turns his shitty camera to where Little is sitting in his car, receiving a rigid middle finger in the air for his trouble. Despite his anger, Mickey obediently moves his car when the deputy asks so he can measure the distances of the skid where the judge's car first started off the road and the indentation it left against the berm. The gouge in the mud is clearly visible now that the tide has started going out. There are bits of glass scattered all over from the judge's wrecked car. Mickey watches as Hernandez measures each major piece of glass, then pick up and package other detritus from where it has fallen.

"I'm leaving," Little calls out to Hernandez, only to have the officer abandon his work and saunter slowly over to Little's car.

"You're the star of the story, Little," Hernandez says. "So I'll give you something to be a star about. I've warned you not to interrupt my investigation. You've not only interfered with an active crime scene, you've also interfered with the investigation after the fact."

Mickey grimaces. The deputy is clearly restating this for the sake of the vehicle camera on the dash of the police car.

"You have the right to remain silent," the deputy begins. "What you say can be used against you. You have the right to have a lawyer present during any questioning by the police. If you can't afford a lawyer, one will be appointed to represent you. If you are not a citizen, you have the right to ask me to notify your embassy. Do you understand these rights?"

Little cocks his head sideways, looking down his nose at Hernandez in amazement. "Don't you *Mirandize* me, you little Mexican prick. You ain't got the balls to arrest Mickey Little."

"Mr. Little, you are under arrest as a material witness." Hernandez says calmly. "I'm putting you in my squad car for your own protection. If what you claim is true, an assailant is still on the loose. I'll call a wrecker to pull your car to the impound lot where you may retrieve it."

"Sure, you're gonna arrest me. You and what army?" Little asks.

"You might want to think before you say anything else. The attacker, if what you say is true, is still out there with a gun. He would know you saw it, if that's what happened, and he might come back for you. My camera in my car is on and has been for the duration. It's recording this conversation, and everything you've done and said since I pulled up. An attack on an officer, impeding the officer's official duty, and evading apprehension are all separate felony charges. I can also handcuff you if you don't follow my direction to get in the back of my squad car, so I can make sure you remain safe as a material witness. That's not a criminal charge, it's for your safety."

Hernandez let Little get his things from his car and closes his own door as Little slides obediently into the locked car, testing the handle and finding it locked.

Through the tinted window, Mickey can see Hernandez go back to his measurements.

CHAPTER ELEVEN:
The Miracle of Surgery

Light floods the close scene around Judd Baker's damaged head. It takes on the effect of a floral wreath of cotton bandanas and paper caps that bend over and around the judge: surgeons, anesthesiologists, nurses, all stacked in order of rank and need for proximity to the patient.

The shaved circle in the center of the judge's head reflects blue green light in this close scene. His pasty face is held down by lines sending liquid in and bringing liquid out. Bright green sheets complete the bouquet effect around the head, floating in the sea of color as if it doesn't have a body.

In addition to the crowd in the OR, a small group look on from an observation window, available for most procedures for the benefit of interested medical students.

This morning, more students than ever make the window look small: the famous Arthur Wade is manning the scalpel and those who must pass his close scrutiny before the end of their school year have gotten the call and dragged themselves out to watch.

One side of the circle below is left open as if to the heavens, creating a window of access to those who look down on this display. Available for many procedures, today the student observation room is standing room only: medical students pile over each other for the view.

Not a word is said.

Throughout the school year, some students haunt this room to see the techniques that will help them hone their own skills when the day comes. Others never come here, not yet acclimated to seeing blood flow so freely.

Today their number fills the audience space for the famous Dr. Wade. The operation is difficult, the chances for success slim. An elevated machine displays a scan of the patient's brain and shows clearly where the bullet is lodged. Someone has tracked the removal course with marks on the screen: the path looks perilous. Another machine has the same image, but the second one seems to be "live."

Not only is Wade demonstrating his skill in this emergency: when he finishes, most of those in that overview room will face him in the classroom. Those who pass his appraisal complete their training. Those who don't, will not, at least not in surgery. His students reverently accept his nod in their direction, and if anything, become even quieter after he enters the arena and takes in each of them in a swift movement of his head, making eye contact and nodding as if he is taking roll.

Like a triumphant Roman emperor coming into the Forum, Wade next reviews his patient, lying before him prepped, waiting, and as comatose as the anesthesiologist can safely make him.

A shower, of sorts—more like a hosing down—preceded the operation and took place well before they moved the patient into this sterile, well-lighted center area. Water sluiced away the mud not matted into hair and careful swabbing took the rest as the patient's hair was shaved and the head sanitized. Wade does not lower his gloved hands to check because he trusts his team.

Eccentric.

Self-possessed.

Religious.

Arthur Wade is one of the few clinical professors who brings prayer into the classroom at that level; and he does so, probably because he is one of the few who can get away with it. Acknowledged to be the best available for brain trauma surgery—and the best in at least his third of the state if not the entire country—Wade's silent colleagues may reject his rhetoric of piety, but no one denies his expertise. And since showmanship does not exceed ability, they give him leave. Given the circumstances of a serious head injury, any one of them would accept the prayer in exchange for the rescue. Wade holds his gloved hands elevated, careful to touch nothing as he paces sure-footedly around the operating table.

"Showtime, folks," he says, leaning into the ear of the anesthesiologist.

Then for his audience, he turns, raises his face, eyes open to make a direct address to his creator, and prays loud enough for each visitor to hear:

"Almighty God, Lord of us all, this patient is in Your Mighty Hands! Guide Your lowly servant to Your Glory and not ours!"

They cannot help but close their eyes as Wade lowers his head and turns back toward his patient.

"Is he for real? Seriously?" an eager first-year, who heard of the rush to the glassed-in enclosure and came to observe, whispers to his seatmate.

"As real as a heart attack," the upperclassman tells him. "Wait until you hear his sermon on God and the brain!"

"Can't wait," the first-year notes.

"Seriously, Dude," the upperclassman cautions. "You'll never look at God or the brain the same way again."

The first year nods politely, thinking that his older colleague might have been at the hospital for a few too many hours without sleep.

"Your brain feels like a bowl of Jello in your hands," the upperclassman recites from memory." It's not heavy, three or four pounds at most. The most complex material we've discovered in the universe, the brain is your mission control center. It drives the operation that is you, gathers dispatches. Each neuron and glia— hundreds or billions of them—is as complicated as an entire city's infrastructure. Each contains the entire human genome and trafficks billions of molecules. Each sends electrical pulses to other cells, up to hundreds of times per second. If you could reduce these trillions of pulses in your brain to a single photon of light, it would blind you. Connected to one another in a network so complex that no human language can describe it, a single cubic centimeter of brain tissue has as many connections as there are stars in the Milky Way Galaxy. The three-to-four-pound organ in your skull—with its pink consistency of Jello—is an alien kind of computational miracle. It is composed of miniaturized self-configuring parts, and it vastly outstrips anything man ever dreamt of building. If you ever feel lazy or dull, take heart: God has made sure you're the busiest, brightest thing on His Planet. The machinery is utterly alien to us, and yet, somehow, it is us."[2]

Below this rarified discussion, the patient, an atheist-leaning agnostic, is in no position to object to being prayed over.

2   David Eagleman, *Incognito, The Secret Lives of the Brain*, Pantheon Books: New York, 211, Chapter One: "There's Someone in My Head, But It's Not Me."

CHAPTER TWELVE:
The Brain

I am working hard here to stay focused.

This body is trying to slip away from me, and that scalpel came so close, so many times to things I need left alone.

I know my man is not all that impressed by prayers and rarified discussion because he's an agnostic of long-standing but I think he wants to go on living and doing good for people.

And clever, he is, but he wants to use this situation to let his emotional self dictate terms to me, his rational self, and frankly, I'm the smarter of this duo.

He holds his own most of the time, but his processes are primitive compared with mine.

But lucky for him: he can go on living without my higher brain.

They've proved that. When people actually lose the part I am, that old primitive codger left over from evolution just charges right up and learns to carry on.

I'm telling you this so you will understand a little bit about my panic; I can't live without his primitive brain.

He's so out of it right now that I'm having a hard time keeping him up with me, but we need to help this doctor!

Why my man seems so dead-set on opening these folders that I keep closed, seems obvious—in this time of crisis, he wants to unearth all those things he feels guilty about as if an apology at this point will smooth out the situation. He forces himself to return to things that cause him colossal depths of guilt.

Why do that?

These things are over.

Let them rest.

Maybe it's human nature to seek redemption, but we need to be up here! Optimistic! Not wandering through the past!

I tell him, but he doesn't listen.

We are not Catholic even in earlier generations, I tell him. So we don't have to suffer Catholic guilt this way.

Nor Baptist for that matter.

I say it and draw a smile.

He knows we never did the religion thing, so if he thinks that might have helped, it's a little too late now.

Show your character and your pride! His primitive brain is totally unforgiving.

Don't embarrass us by pretending you, my man, weren't affected at the time when those very sincere church people marched against you because you ruled for that girl.

I was embarrassed for them—*praying the girl would die and go straight to hell because she wanted to scrape that athlete's sperm out of her uterus.*

Given the fact he had no right or permission to put it there, she had a point.

And they didn't appreciate my man telling her she could do what she wanted with her own body.

Thinking girl that she was, she slipped away to Europe. Enrolled in school.

She was already studying art history by the time they reached her with the result.

And then how they gathered around that little you-know-what who was getting away with his poor choices under the guise that he was on the side of God and the angels trying to save his baby's life?

Maybe he should be made to think about where he puts it and the risks to others of just being in his company.

Judd! I snap at him again.

He's after another one.

He played around a little.

What the hay?

They all did in the sixties.

You need to rest, I say.

I open the folder to Austin when he was just a kid, Freshman at UT and fell in love with an angel.

Before the others.

A sweet, adorable virgin who wanted to go all the way with him, to make it a special experience for both of them.

And they did.

And I loved it.

He always settles down when he thinks of that pretty little thing who we both fell in love with.

The first love of our life.

I keep her in the special folder in that special place where the true loves of one's life are stored in the heart.

He stumbles.

These days he can never remember her name; and I won't help him as I try to keep his thoughts on her just a little bit longer, requiring him to search back in time to those long nights in Austin.

. . . walking through the UT campus

. . .stopping beneath every shady overhang to hug and kiss.

I, retrieving it, hold it away to keep him searching.

You know what the secret is. It's the essence of what he felt for her that he doesn't want to lose, that fresh feeling of first love for them both.

I wonder sometimes how she ended up.

I am no more capable than you of seeing into the future. The brain can't remember what hasn't occurred yet. It's why you get lost in parking garages if you don't pay attention and tell me what to remember!

My man is a coward and worse when it comes to women, love. With the needs of the body, he's even worse.

I wonder if he just fears he will have to pay a price for experiencing joy and excitement.

Probably, I think.

But we jump right in anyway.

I sometimes spend a lot of energy just daring him to take a chance.

His blood pressure is dropping.

I fly him over Washington, DC, the one and the only place in the world that I know will send him into spasms of high blood pressure.

Two years only.

That's all he could stand.

When I saw what those bastards had in their cerebral toolboxes, I wanted to puke for America.

Like all the rest, he went there thinking that they were sure to offer him the prize—the one with the white house attached to it.

Doris put a quick end to that daydream.

No way, she said. This is bad enough for a lifetime.

He is struggling from the doctor's hand, threatening to boycott the remainder of this show.

I open her folder and let Doris out.

She takes one look at him and places a firm hand on each cheek.

Doris was always a little too bossy for me.

Even now, I feel the threat from her mere presence.

But I have to admit it: I yearned at times to have a conversation with her other brain!

All of that feeling changed when she lay dying. How horrible that was and how robust the pain made even more so because she was not the type to groan or whimper or let you know what was going on with her.

I know she did it to spare him!

And that's why I also came close to quitting on him when he insisted on sharing his infidelities with her. Why then? That is the type of thing a coward does—not a Judd Baker.

She asked me, he says.

She said she wanted to know.

And I told her.

I loved her too much to lie to her by then.

What did she say? I ask.

She surprised us both.

I thought I was soaring in flight with a romantic adventure with you, she said, but I didn't see that it was more like tripping and falling over my own feet into a Willie Nelson nightmare.

Have you listened to very many of those so-called country songs? She asks, and I think she is talking to me.

Men can't get any lower and that is their music.

And are they ever so proud of such low-life treatment of their women.

Mom, you can't leave him to date that woman! Laura Ann said, loading on the pressure for a woman who didn't need any more of it.

Please, Laura Ann; I'm dead and dying, Doris pleaded.

Leave me be.

If he wants to trash the only good name left in Texas politics, let him do it. You only live once, child.

Thinking of Doris in those long months in which she was dead and dying, he would have walked miles on hot asphalt to avoid the feelings of those moments, but death had moved in and hovered over us until she let it have its way.

I feel her presence now and know that she is extending her life by managing his.

I felt at the time she just didn't want to leave him, helpless as he always appeared to be.

He always needed Doris to tell him what to do, and even now when her control should be just a memory, she picks up her role dutifully. "I'm in there," she says, in a more loving voice, as she leans over his shaved scalp and brushes kisses across his forehead.

"There, inside your head," she insisted.

"You've got to fight."

"We need you."

Laura Ann, she means.

And Tripp.

. . .

This doctor is probably good,
But he is keeping me on the run.

When that scalpel gets too close, I do what I have to do. I shrink up real small and move as far away from that knife as I can.

Judd doesn't know come 'ere from sic 'em at this point but I see and feel it all and rush to reconnect the things this guy is cutting because he can't know where he is and even if he did, he can't see these parts that he is clipping that fly away as if seeking freedom on the outside.

I open Doris' folder again, hoping she will help me calm him while I correct and reattach these mess-ups.

I can't win this battle without you, I tell her.

He's fighting to call it quits.

Is that what you want? I have him ask her. You ready for me there? He asks.

"No," she says, "you still have to do your penance, little man."

"And Laura Ann needs you for Tripp."

And I don't, I have total freedom here.

I need for you to take these ropes off, Doris, he says very plaintively. They have me tied.

She looks at me.

I can't win this battle without you, I tell her again. It is true because he and his 10 percent are wishing wildly to be let go and that would be it. He is tired and old and frustrated and doesn't believe he can take it anymore.

But WE CAN! I scream. WE CAN!

Struggling to remove the bindings holding him down, he finally gets her attention.

Take him to that place I beg her. Please just a little more now. They almost have the damage sewed up. He stretches against the bindings but her hands take hold on each side of his face.

Why are they doing this? he asks but Doris doesn't answer; she just holds on tighter.

The doctor's entourage moves in closer, their actions panicked and direction more an assault on him with their last probes.

I do all I can do.

I lift his spirit away from them and let it hover near the ceiling looking down.

I'm still busy here.

He is on his own up there until I finish supervising what this doctor is doing!

Doris looks his way. Once more, he is in the jon boat with Tripp on the first morning.

And the child, as serious about this voyage as Admiral Byrd was his, looks at Judd and says,

"Grandpa, do fish go to heaven when they die?"

And Judd looks bewildered.

The time for agnosticism does not apply when this child is

*concerned with an issue and the child turns to him and the morning
sun comes through the blonde curls that stand out around his angelic
face like a halo.*

And Judd takes a deep breath.

It's interesting you should ask, he says.

I asked Mom but she said to ask you.

Ah ha, Judd says, his suspicions confirmed.

*I guess the answer is known to us all, Tripp, he says, using his
very best scholarly tone.*

*If I were God, I would definitely have this beautiful creature in
my heaven.*

Me too, Grandpa! Me too!

CHAPTER THIRTEEN:
The REAL Lawyer

"Little Phoebe is in trouble again," Bull MacPearson growls into Hurley's ear. "Might be big."

It is not the first time Augustus MacPearson has called Hurley Brown before daybreak; and it's not the first time Hurley has grunted a *Yes Sir, I'll get right on that* before rolling over to grab a handful of titty and go immediately back to sleep. This time, in addition to the pleasant handful, he's got one knee crooked into an ass that feels so good he wishes he could remember whose it is.

He wakes that morning with a mouth on his dick.

"What time is it?" he asks and the girl dutifully removes her mouth and answers.

"Good God Almighty," he complains. "Don't you ever get enough? It's only been two hours!"

She giggles and goes back to her work. This amiable lawyer has agreed to cut a thousand dollars from his fee for each time she does a nice favor for him. She's sure been keeping her end of the bargain up.

One thing Hurley learned in his early days as a lawyer: working out legal fees often gets him consistent and sometimes very high-quality pussy. And when it comes to pussy, Hurley is even willing to lower his standards sometimes. He remembers his Grandaddy telling him when he complained about being sent off to Texas A&M, "Even a dog can get the job done."

That sure ended up being the truth. And now, the women there are not only first quality in the looks department but ace all the tests. The only downside to pussy from whatever source: it doesn't pay the rent.

But there are no taxes to be paid on it and that is a good thing, he thinks, knowing he will always rationalize the issue in favor of a continued supply.

Hurley swings his legs off the bed and stands up, stretching.

"I gotta pay the rent, Babydoll," he says.

And, as if on autopilot the girl gets up and heads for the kitchen, making the coffee and bringing it back up to his room to hold the cup to his lips when he steps out of the shower.

Awake finally, he calls the Detention Center.

"Why didn't you call me last night before PC-ing my little girl?" he yells indignantly into the telephone.

The dispatcher pauses before answering. "Again, Hurley? She had an attorney. Judge appointed one."

"Well, that ain't gonna do," he says. "Who'd he name?"

"Alexandra McLeod, goes by Shadow. She's new."

"Well, that's nothing that can't be changed. Sounds like a made-up name to me. Ya'll check her out?"

"She's actually pretty good, Hurley. Even came to court when notified at three in the morning."

"I had something going on," he says. "She can be released."

"Kid may not want her to. They *bonded*."

"They can un-bond," Hurley says flatly. "Commissioner hired me."

"Well imagine that. One of the big boys is taking an interest in one of our little juvie cases," the dispatcher's voice practically drips with condescending Southern charm.

This dispatcher, Evie, knows him too well, though she seems to like him well enough. Hurley can be an underhanded bastard when he needs to be. If he needs to cover himself for not being on hand for the girl's hearing, he'll lay the blame on Evie or Hernandez or anyone handy.

"It was just PC," Evie adds. Judge is coming back at one for the real thing."

"Well, that's good. I guess that means I don't have to raise a stink against the bitch after all." Lilly Pruser draws most of his anger these days. Hurley has a visceral dislike for Lilly. Not that the bitch wouldn't be called a looker in Hurley's estimation, but even when she knows Hurley is right on the law, she looks right through him like cellophane and says: *Denied.*

"Wasn't the B," Evie responds calmly.

"Then who?"

"Judd Baker. Was on for two more days, but not now. Somebody'll be here for docket at one. Be here."

Hurley hangs up the phone and nuzzles his face in the thick, strawberry blonde hair of his latest DWI client.

What is her name? he thinks. *Oh, yeah, Brandie the DWI. Brandie S-something. Brandie Sweetie? No, that's not it. Oh right, just Sweet. Brandie Sweet. That's gotta be made-up.*

"Is your last name for real?" He asks.

"No, darlin', neither name is real. Now who's hunting?"

"Not so, darlin'," Hurley whispers. He loves women, especially young ones with that honey red hair. Even when it comes from a bottle, he loves it. "If I had another night with you, girl, I'd stroke for sure."

She laughs as he finishes off his coffee and hands the cup to her.

"We gotta change that name of yours before we go to trial," he says. "No jury's gonna believe that's real. They'll laugh us out of court."

"Changed it to this to dance," she says. "You can't change it now while I have charges pending." She has been down this road before. Her profession draws cops like magnets and they all stop her, sometimes just to talk and catch a number.

"That's the DA's problem," he says. "I won't object when they replead the indictment to get the name right. About tonight," he starts but she takes over.

"I know," she says. "Clear out early, like now. The little lady's coming home."

"The War Department's on the way," Hurley says, as if saddened. Rosemary has been in India for three weeks with friends, soaking up Hindu shit like crazy. She must be putting something up her nose over there if what's already been delivered is an indication. Curry. Silk. Herbal baths. Boxes of silk and gold braid. No doubt, she is planning another renovation of their turn of the century mansion.

"The whole town knows about your *habits*, Hurley. How can she not know?" the girl asks, leaning against his chest for a goodbye hug.

"She might for sure," Hurley mumbles into the girl's hair. "Maybe she just doesn't mind sharing me."

"Turns a blind eye, more like," the girl says. "She's no fool, you know."

"Breaking news," a young woman's voice interrupts their farewell as they step into the kitchen. Hurley grabs her carry bag and watches as Brandie goes automatically to the sink to wash out their mugs. She dries them and returns them to where they belong. Hurley smiles. Women like him so much they try to remove all traces of their having been here.

The newscast continues, "Galveston County retired Judge Judd Baker is undergoing surgery at this time for serious head injuries in what might have been a single car accident near the County's Detention Center for Juveniles. There is no word yet on why the judge was on that road at three in the morning, the estimated time of the accident. Further details to follow as we hear more."

CHAPTER FOURTEEN:
The Brain

I leave him as he marches.

I know the scene and he does too, but he can't quite get there.

I opened the folder because they took out the bullet and sewed him up and he is trying to wake up.

But now he takes in the image the canvas body gives him and shudders...

I let him be.

I want him distracted and so far, the carnage he is caught up in is doing its job.

He and Doris studied that painting by Picasso, who Doris said she doesn't like, but can't stop thinking about.

In Europe, they said at the time, it was so powerful, it marked them forever.

It did. It is a nightmare, and I let him get caught up in it.

I figure that if I can just keep him plodding through this nightmare, he at least will give me a rest.

The doc got that bullet out.

But it was not as easy as he thought it would be.

He managed it after a struggle; and I think my man would have been gone had that bullet not finally given in and slid out at the doc's urging.

I just hope there's not too much damage along that path in the aftermath, but we are swelling.

I can almost feel the fluid pumping in and blowing out veins and valves: not a good feeling.

The nightmare of the painting was the only experience we ever had sufficient to pull him out for a time like this.

I never realized pain could be this bad, but I feel it spreading in waves of hot flashes throughout our body.

He heaves and they rush to pump something else into us.

He tries to escape but they pull him down and lay ice blankets over us.

I wonder if a body can explode from that quick temperature change. The ice starts its work immediately.

In our mind, the surface of the painting absorbs the cold and the heat. When he tries to plod across it to get away, the thickly applied paint tries to go with him, sticking to his feet, lifting and stretching and pulling against him enough to make him slip and fall into the picture, overturning a pieta with its suffering mother and dead child, knocking a horse over that has already been sacrificed and given up its entrails, narrowly missing the horns of a bull whose tail is dissected and on fire above his head.

And there he sees once more the eye that never closes, still staring at him, as angry as the one in the banged-up old truck.

He sees the bombs falling and more planes in the distance dropping so many that each window sprouts fire and jumping women and children.

And then he sees Doris trying to put out the light that is the eye, but it burns still even after she breaks it into many pieces.

He feels the heat of the fallen horse and its entrails that are spread around him and the flower in the fallen soldier's hand.

Judd wants to touch his own head.

He needs suddenly to see if it is still there.

"Did they take my brain, Doris?" he calls out.

She looks at him and strikes the burning light again.

"My head is empty," he tells her and he does not like the fact that he comes across as whining.

He floats through and around a garden of swords, broken, everywhere flaming tongues of them and women.

"Can't they stop screaming?" He asks, and hopes it isn't him.

And Doris is an angel now but she is leaving him again.

"Don't go Doris; you're better than this!"

"I don't know who you think you are, little man," Doris says, and turns away from him.

You've still got some penance to do.

"I thought I had an Annie-Hall-Woody-Allen-love adventure going with you in this marriage," she says. "And instead, it's more like falling into a Willie Nelson song, all sad and repentant."

"I got a long list of real good reasons," his brain says for him, proving it is still there.

"For all the things I've done.

I've got a picture in the back of my mind;

Of what I've lost and what I've won..."[3]

Doris' laugh is a mighty burst as she swings the staff she carries over the scene.

Doris fades as she calls out and he realizes he is alone.

She is gone.

Forever, she is gone?

Why live? He thinks about it and knows his brain is working and sees that he does want to go on living.

---

3   Willie Nelson *Live in Austin Disc*
.

CHAPTER FIFTEEN:
The Reporter

Mickey Little slams his fingers hard against his keyboard, causing it to rattle against his dinged and bent metal-topped desk. When he had stalked into the office, his colleagues scattered like salt from pepper to the outer edges of the newsroom, leaving Mickey to his vortex of fury in the center.

To say that he's angry is an understatement. Mickey Little is compelled into a wild madness. His wiry, graying hair stands on end, still unwashed from his overnight ordeal in the jail. Unshaven, he looks dissipated and old. His fingers, more bent than usual, are swollen with arthritic inflammation, setting off painful shooting stars as each finger strikes a key.

He doesn't wince once.

Mickey Little is on a familiar mission, the blood surging within him.

That fucking Mexican uniform won't get away with what he's done. The story of the year falls into his lap and he has that arrogant deputy telling him he's only being let go on his own recognizance— the nerve! *"Call your lawyer to get the camera and disk with the pictures back."* Unbelievable.

Little takes a long swig of coffee, thinking of his next line. He can fix this, Mickey thinks, with just a few written words.

This reporter witnessed a truck drive a Judge's car off the road this morning, causing serious head injuries to the judge.

Then this reporter was placed under arrest as a material witness: a thin excuse to detain him from a biased police officer. The investigative officer, one Felipe Hernandez, treated this reporter worse than a common criminal and made no effort to pursue the assailant.

The crime this reporter witnessed occurred close to 3 a.m. this morning while following up on a confidential tip that an under-aged granddaughter of powerful Galveston County Commissioner Augustus "Bull" MacPearson was going to be secretly released from the Galveston County Detention Center for juveniles, despite the fact that she gained access to a loaded gun and killed another teenager at a drunken orgy at her mother's house.

This reporter was traveling behind retired Senior District Court Judge Judd Baker as he left the Detention Center where he had been filling in for judge Lilly Pruser, who was not available to perform her duties. After finding probable cause, or sufficient evidence of a crime for a trial, Baker ordered the girl to stay in the Detention center overnight.

When a speeding pick-up truck ran the judge off the road, this reporter was unable to rescue the judge or stop the crime, but took pictures of the events as they occurred, even recording the license plate to help authorities locate the perpetrator.

Investigative officer Hernandez, rather than appreciating this reporter's contributions, locked him in the back of his squad car as if he, and not the pick-up driver who left the scene of the accident, was the perpetrator. The attack of the pick-up against the judge's much smaller Prius sent the judge into surgery for a life-threatening head injury. The judge underwent surgery at Galveston's Sealy Hospital, which refused to make a statement for this reporter and the public about the judge's condition at this reporter's deadline.

Judd Baker is the District Court Judge who retired after this reporter revealed that Baker signed an order allowing an under-aged child to be considered an adult so she could kill her baby against the wishes of the baby's father, a former outstanding Ball High School quarterback. Both mother and father were minors at the time. The boy's parents sued to stop the abortion. The girl's parents joined that suit. This entire community joined the boy's campaign and marched on Baker's office, surrounded the Courthouse with a circle of prayer, and held a 24-hour vigil outside Sealy Hospital where the girl was believed to be seeking the procedure. Unknown to all, the girl had skipped away to Europe and killed the baby, staying in Europe to complete her education with the help of Planned Parenthood, that nefarious abortion service in this country. Judge Baker retired at the height of public outpouring of support for the young father, about whom Baker opined that not being married to the girl and not having yet filed an Affidavit of Paternity with the state, the young father had no rights or say in the matter. The Texas Legislature in its next session made a major overhaul of the legislation, allowing girls to bypass parental permission for an abortion if they showed the maturity necessary for a District Court Judge to remove their legal disabilities. Notice to the parents is now required.

Coming back to yet another travesty visited upon this reporter, a greater crime was then carried out against this reporter by an uninformed worker from the Detention Center, Felipe Hernandez, who violated this reporter's constitutionally protected First Amendment right of a free press by seizing this reporter's camera and arresting this reporter. Hernandez excused his conduct by stating that this reporter's camera contained evidence of a crime, claiming that this reporter could be a suspect for all he knew.

This reporter agrees that Hernandez doesn't know much. He cavalierly denounced this reporter's important Constitutional rights— the First Amendment be damned he said—by imposing a prior restraint on the press, by seizing this reporter's camera, and by making the false accusation that this reporter was involved in the accident. It is the worst abuse by state action under the color of lawful authority that this reporter has ever heard of in the history of the free press.

The *Enterprise* directed its lawyers to file suit against the worker, individually; the judge he works for, Lilly Pruser, who was not performing her judicial duties for the people at the time all of this was going down; the Detention Center; and the county and city officials for the egregious prior restraint on the press. *Enterprise* lawyers assure the public that this reporter and the *Enterprise* would have protected what the Detention Center worker described as evidence of a possible crime.

✎

Despite "No Smoking" signs, one of which was placed by a co-worker on his cubicle wall, Little leans back in his chair and lights a cigarette, blowing smoke up and over the wall into his cubicle mate's part of the room. He re-reads his intro. He finds his lapse into personal opinion excusable in the seventh paragraph and knows that his loyal readers will know just how justly irked he is that yet another taxpayer-paid-public-employee has kept information from the public.

He picks up his ringing phone, barking his customary "Little!"

"Little," Felipe Hernandez says into the phone. "You can come get what's left of your camera if you want it."

"What do you mean, *what's left of it?*"

"It downloaded real well to the department's system. We also have Olympus-friendly software."

"And my pictures?"

"They're still there, what you can see from them. Don't give up your day job though if you're expecting awards for them," Hernandez says.

Little feels his blood pressure rise: "You destroyed my pictures, you worthless-sack-of-shit-Mexican!"

"No need to get racist about it, Little!"

"Just like you to pull the race card when you get yourself in trouble, *Felipe*. It won't work. I'm clean on race. I worked the Valley before coming here."

"Yeah, you can take the Anglo out of the Valley, but you can't take the Valley out of the Anglo," Hernandez says.

"Go fuck yourself, Dickless," Little says.

Little can hear the smile as Hernandez hangs up the phone.

Feels a twinge of angst.

Even if the *Enterprise* is on the verge of folding, Mickey Little lives in tall cotton until it happens. As long as he stays in the state of Texas, he always has a job. People in Texas know he stands up for what's right and just. From a reporter's standpoint, he's in his prime.

Knows how to do the job.

Knows just which words to use to avoid libel and slander. In fact, things have never been so good for him. He has an editor who leaves him alone for the most part, and has even protected him on one important matter. His editor says he doesn't want his paper brought down by foolish mistakes. In the Valley and other places, Little often left just before the lawsuits resolved, but he has learned how to dodge future bullets. He also knows Hernandez has no way of knowing that Confidentiality Agreements are ironclad ways to keep your secrets.

"You're gonna find out," he mutters to his now empty phone, "as they say, it's hard to defend against someone whose employers buy ink by the barrel." He thinks about what he'll do with it if he gets that twenty million this time. Money might be secondary to the crusade for Mickey, but it's also been a lot scarcer lately. A nice fat check from a wrongful arrest suit would set him up nice.

CHAPTER SIXTEEN:
The Deputy

Felipe drops his pen on his desk and lets his head sink onto his folded arm. He's been on duty twelve hours and sees twelve more ahead.

From the judge's Chamber, he hears Shadow McLeod snoring as if comfortably and deeply asleep. How can she sleep so peacefully, with all this excitement surrounding everyone?

She agreed to stay, rather than try to drive back to her house on the West End of the island. She lives even further out the island than Baker and in a much less impressive cottage.

"That might be a good thing, given what happened to Baker," he mumbles as Evie walks up and puts a paper towel and a cup with steam rising off it under his nose.

"At least I got to shower," he tells her.

"Well, you had to; you were totally covered in mud and highway oil. What a mess!"

"Now I have to get my car cleaned out."

"I already had them pick it up," Evie says.

"You are too good to me," he tells her. "Thanks," he says, indicating the coffee. He picks up the cup, sipping off the top.

"Wow! That'll wake you up," he says, taking his pen and using it to once more dial Pruser's cell, using his desk phone, which is large and bulky. If he could just get a hold of her, his day would get so much easier. He knows how Lilly tackles problems.

Lilly went to Missouri to see her sick mom because her last conversation with her mom scared her. Her mom is sick, and is getting old. Lilly's probably on her way back now though, since she's not picking up. She probably drove through the night and is trying to push through the last few hours this morning to get her kids back home quicker.

This is the first time Lilly is making the trip without her husband around to help out. Felipe doesn't know how they're doing with the separation: he and Lilly might talk about travel plans, but they don't talk about anything that personal. He's glad she's getting out of the marriage though. Her husband seems like a do-nothing kind of guy.

He dials Lilly's number one more time, unsurprised when it goes to voicemail. Her phone must be off or lost somewhere in or under a seat, buzzing away every time he calls. He can't blame her. How could anyone anticipate a case like this?

"You better watch yourself with that reporter, Fee Lo," Evie says, giving him both coffee and advice. She too has been here with him twelve hours and she'll stay until he leaves. She sent Betsy home at daybreak, but Evie will be the last man standing; she will not leave Fee Lo to face it alone.

He takes another sip and smiles.

"Fixed like I like it," he says, licking his parched lips. He loves these occasional long shifts with Evie.

"I know, I know." She says. "So good you'd like to marry me twice if I weren't twice your age."

"Age wouldn't stop me," he swears, taking a longer draw from the cup.

"Whatever you say, lover boy." Evie grimaces as the conversation takes a more serious turn. "You don't want to hear what the dickless reporter's been saying about you."

"Fucking Mickey Little." Felipe says. "I ain't afraid of a bastard like him."

"He can spin a yarn," she warns.

"I know, and his version won't be even close to the truth."

"Exactly. He does it with or without facts and he'll burn you if he can," she says. "You know who's coming in for the kid at one?"

"Yeah, but she's already got a lawyer. Shadow's still here, she's waiting for Phoebe to calm down."

"That gal won't fly for a MacPearson," Evie says, shuffling back toward the front entrance where she is supposed to be managing the gate.

"Make sure they compensate her triple time for coming in at three this morning while Hurley '*addressed other matters*'."

"Sure, boss. You just be ready for Hurley and Little," she calls out over her shoulder as she walks out of the room. "Hurley's already on a tear because we didn't call him—says he's been tapped by the old man."

"Cakewalk," Felipe says. He laughs cynically to himself at Evie's warning about Little and Hurley together on another crusade. They're a pair for sure. The last time they teamed up, they caused Judd Baker to step down early from the bench. Hurley has a habit of forming a vendetta against any judge who rules against his client, which Baker did.

He suspects Lilly will be their next target—the signs are already there. It would hardly be shocking. Hurley hates her personally, and Little just doesn't like women. *Some enterprising soul should find a way to bring those two down,* Felipe thinks to himself. Hurley's only gotten this far because of his connections.

Felipe never worries too much when one of his kids gets "the best lawyer in town" to represent them. If Hurley was that good, he would have been at the Center hours ago, when Phoebe was brought before the judge.

The judges who handle the Juvenile Court, Lilly and Tamara Brown, both keep lists of names of new young lawyers and the older ones they rotate through to represent these kids. Some show up daily looking for work. Some are good and really know their stuff. Some are jackasses who'll plead out anybody just to get their pay quicker. Felipe keeps his own private list. The lazy ones move quickly to the bottom of it, because he is often the one who has to clean up the fall out.

Despite the disadvantages, it really is the best option. Hell, there's no good place for kids in trouble in the whole state of Texas. Theirs is the best and it still feels like a prison.

As a child of the valley, Felipe has a vested interest in his job that others might not have had. He has his own past with a Juvenile Detention Center. He owes his job here to Lilly. When he told her about his record, she told him that she expected him to remember his experiences and hired him on the spot. She relies on him in a unique way. He can understand the kids they see in the Center due to his background, but can also be trusted to always work within the rules.

Growing up in Texas, which for all its diversity can have a clear racist bent, has taught Felipe when to let the shitty comments slide off his back. Tonight was different. He surprised himself: usually he prefers to fly under the radar and not make too many waves. But when he saw the judge hanging upside down in that car with dickless Little snapping pictures—an image that keeps coming back to mind—his anger overwhelmed him. It might not have been smart to pick a fight with Mickey Little, but it was a long time coming.

Felipe just hopes his actions haven't hurt Lilly's chances in the upcoming election. She's been incredibly stressed about it all, but the position couldn't go to a worthier candidate. Young, female, highly qualified—Lilly's winning this election would be good for their community. He won't fail to support her, whatever happens.

But he can't bend now, even if it means inviting a vendetta. He's heard the rumors about Dickless. As of tonight, he's seen him up close and personal. His limping gait, caused by a case of polio in childhood, reminds Felipe of an old horror movie he and his childhood friend Pedro sneakily watched when they were young. The slap of the villain's wooden leg terrified him as a kid. He can't deny, a part of him is listening nervously for the slap of Little's platform support shoe in the hall.

Felipe isn't afraid of Mickey Little, but only a fool wouldn't be a little nervous, being on his bad side. As far as he's concerned, Little is truly a disgusting human being who must be hiding some real darkness. He can't understand how other people admit Little into their lives.

The crusade, which Hurley directed at Baker, was a convergence of a lot of things that just happened to come together. Little was still new to town at the time and needed a cause; he jumped on Hurley's bandwagon against Baker. Even Hurley expressed surprise over the vitriol Little threw on an incessant basis at the judge, until Baker basically told them to take the job and shove it. Hurley had all but offered to shake hands with Baker and go back to being friends, but Baker wasn't willing to swallow the insult and stay. He had just lost his life companion to cancer, a slow and painful death. With his retirement maxed out, he had no good reason to stay.

Like most people in town, Felipe never had a problem with Hurley, who was more or less regarded as the community's likeable fool; *he's our own problem*, folks would say. Hurley Brown's mother was the town's major for a decade: a dear old woman who was beloved by most. Folks were frankly proud when Hurley came home to practice law. The courthouse crowd helped him through his breaking-in hurdles and still overlook his missed deadlines.

Sometimes, those who favored him would give him a well-placed smile in the presence of a juror or two, so they would know he was a favorite son. Hell, some still did, although Fee Lo thinks Hurley has pushed the envelope so many times with so many people that it is becoming harder and harder to find folks who will look the other way. He came out of the Baker affair muddy and, for some, like Felipe, Hurley will never be able to dust off the dried residue from that experience.

It left the same bad taste for many.

Hardly anybody that Felipe knows is free from the baggage of life and he recognizes his own scrapes that left lasting scars. Hell, he knows Lilly has a bunch, most related now to her heartfelt determination to escape from her marriage and move her old man out on good terms, which is not easy for a woman to do. As long as he didn't want to go, he would threaten to leave and take the kids and it scared her to death. Some say he's on another track now and plans to run against her if she wins this bench. He thinks the public will return her home to take care of the kids, which he thinks is the way it ought to be.

Felipe hopes the world is changing enough to prevent that.

Lilly's only problem where Felipe is concerned is that she just sometimes refuses to face the music and dance. But, he thinks, that if that's your only or your worst problem, it ain't so bad.

He hears little Phoebe call out something rude sounding yet again from the back. He thinks about getting up, but decides there's two women who can take care of her and stays put. He puts his head on his desk and the image of Phoebe Sunshine MacPearson floats before him. Scrawny, ill-looking, pale, bony, and deprived looking, *poor little rich girl*, he thinks, *most likely responding to what she's been denied rather than all that she's been given.*

CHAPTER SEVENTEEN:
The Granddaughter

"Okay, little miss, listen up," Hurley tells Phoebe. "We're gonna go before that judge out there and even though she's not the one you called an asshole, you're gonna apologize to her for the judge you did call an asshole."

"Never," the girl says defiantly.

"Don't you *never* me, young lady. You're wanting out of here so bad and I'm gonna do it to shut you up; but if you don't cooperate and do what I tell you to, I'll tell them to bring you back here and put you under that bunk until you're ready to be sent to the big house for good."

"You can't talk to me like that. I don't need you anyway, I already have a lawyer and *she's* really nice."

"She was for an emergency. I'm taking her place. I'll pay your other lawyer for your Grandpa, who told me to do what I can and do what I think is best for you."

"They took my panties…"

"You were drunk and high. You could've hanged yourself with them."

"And my bra."

"Same thing," he says. "I would have done that myself."

"No one who knows me thinks I'd do something like that. I have a lot to live for, asshole."

"Don't start that with me either," Hurley tells her. "This ain't my first rodeo with you, young lady. I know what a lying little skank you are."

"That was years ago," she says, glaring.

"Not that many years," Hurley says. "Two to be exact."

"I can't help it if I have to tell the truth and people don't like it."

"I can't trust a word that comes out of your mouth. I wouldn't believe you telling me anything but your name."

She lifts her chin. "And I don't trust you either," she says. "You lie about everything, all the time."

"Yeah, that's my job. If I had to tell the truth you'd be in jail for life!"

"Clean up your own house," she says, sounding as preachy as those nuts with signs on street corners.

"And you're gonna make a serious effort to clean up your act, young lady. This is not your *ordinary* fuck-up. This isn't like me getting you off for stealing thongs from Neiman's. You shot that girl from close range. She not only died, you messed her face up so bad her family can't even have an open casket funeral."

"She asked for it."

Phoebe's pout causes her lower lip to jut out defiantly. She looks about twelve years old, sulking in the oversized sweater. Her greasy hair stands out around her round, pasty white face. She has tattoos peeking out of one sleeve, something delicate-looking with tendrils that wrap around her blue-veined arm. But she looks ill. Sick. Surely coldly sober at this point, her wide, glassy eyes give her a look of being permanently stoned or drunk. Her play-acted indignation doesn't have quite the effect it might if she wasn't such a pitiful-looking creature.

"Really," he says. Hurley turns away for a moment. He considers his own exposure, in here alone with Phoebe, who says anything to get what she wants.

Outside the hallway is empty.

"Goddamn it, Phoebe. You shot and killed your best friend. Daughter of your mama's best friend. That situation is not gonna change! Don't you feel *any* remorse?"

"Get over it!" she tells him. "She had it coming."

"Lord, child, nobody has that coming."

"She did," Phoebe says, hitting his shoulder with a balled-up fist.

"Whatever you feel she's done to you, nobody named you judge, jury, and executioner to set the time of someone's departure from this life. I'm gonna sign a waiver to get you psyched. You need to get some serious help before we deal with this."

"You mean you're not letting me go home?"

"You can leave, but at some point, you have to check yourself into a lock-down facility to get some psych treatment before I take this case to a jury."

"I'll call Poppi," she threatens.

"So will I," Hurley tells her, leveling his most severe stare in her direction. So will I, darlin'."

He knocks against the door and after the deputy, Evie Lane, opens it, asks: "Is the judge on the bench?"

"Not till one. Maybe a little later even. She was traveling all night to get here. You hear about Baker?"

"I did. They know who did it?"

"They think they do. That *Enterprise* reporter got some pictures they're trying to blow up to get a plate number."

"Keep her where she can't talk to nobody," Hurley tells the deputy. "Leave her right here if you can and I'll be back at one."

"I have to take her back. Center rules. She must be given lunch even if she won't eat it. I'll bring her up early if you want to see her again before she sees the judge."

"I've got some stuff to arrange. Just keep her where you can get to her fast if you will. I'll owe you."

"She's got another lawyer," Evie tells him. "They seem bonded. The only cooperation we get out of her is when that lawyer's with us."

"She can bond with her all she wants, in fact, but she ain't breaking up my deal."

"She stayed all night to help with her. She didn't leave this morning waiting for the girl to come around."

"That's *her* problem," Hurley says. "She'll get paid if that's the issue. Phoebe can have more than one lawyer; I'm the real one."

"I think Shadow's gonna ask the judge to let her stay. She doesn't like your technique for some reason, Hurley. Maybe she's heard how you insult us all as being beneath you."

And at that precise moment, the gate makes its customary squeal on opening and a sleepy-eyed redhead stumbles into the hallway.

"Deputy," the rumpled lawyer says. "I thought I asked you not to let anyone talk to my client. Especially not someone who would come in here and make vicarious admissions of counsel suggesting that my client is guilty so loudly it would wake up a dead body!"

"That's true, Miss McLeod. You gave me those instructions, but he said they didn't mean anything because he is Phoebe's *real* lawyer, hired by the commissioner."

"Well, I was appointed by the judge to do this job and that takes precedence. Sir, we have not met. I'm Shadow McLeod."

Hurley looks McLeod over, straightening to his full height. She's tall for a woman, almost but not quite as tall as he is. He ignores her outstretched hand: he has no interest in playing nice.

"The court-appointed lawyer. Well, thank you for filling in until I could get here, but you're good to leave now. I'll make sure you're compensated for your time," he says.

"Oh, I'm not going anywhere. The judge appointed me: you have no authority to send me away. And Phoebe has a right to zealous representation of counsel that believes in her. Last I checked, the Constitution says she's innocent until proven guilty. Maybe remember that before you go declaring her guilty for everybody to hear."

Hurley glares at her. Who does this woman think she is, challenging him? He leans back into the room to give Phoebe one last instruction: *"Keep your mouth shut!"* He starts to storm away, but the other lawyer reaches out a hand to stop him.

"Look Mr. Brown, I'm going to ask you, sincerely, don't mess up my client's chances of getting justice due to some warped support you may have for Tuttle. It's clear that he's at least partly responsible for this crime, and the whole world knows it. You've got your hands full there. Leave this case to me."

Hurley mutters "We'll see about that," and shoulders past. The door makes its usual slow and squeaky passage behind him as he storms away.

Later, Hurley sucks in a deep breath as he mounts the steps in his turn-of-the-century mansion in the city's historic district. In keeping with the house's prior spirit, his wife decorated it with an only slightly trashy faux-Victorian look. Hurley has to give her that: Rosemary can take crap and dress it up like Godiva chocolates. He loves the house, and he loves Rosemary's delightful combinations of kitsch and quality that are a little bit like Rosemary herself.

Hurley drops his briefcase by the door and takes the heavily carpeted front stairs in a trot. In some respects, he and Rosemary have created a drama that both perform on behalf of *The Marriage*. When either travels—Rosemary far more often than he—an obligatory performance greets the absent one's return. It has its purpose, and both are content with the half-sincere reunions. He peeps his head around the door, knowing that if she throws something at him, she's found panties or something else that was not hers lying around. Women tend to do that kind of thing to Hurley, he thinks by accident more than plan; but such distinctions do not affect the lovely Rosemary's reactions. The coast seems clear, and he bounds into the red-and-gold-tasseled-room and spreads his arms wide, singing in a rich baritone:

"Darlin, your loving husband is home and primed to pleasure you!"

"Oh Hurley," the lovely Rosemary says, running in from the shower, hair springing into a frizzy mess when she released it from the shower cap, eye make-up run into black circles around wide blue eyes, and tits sticking out as proud as Dallas over the towel she wraps around herself at the waist, leaving them free. "You're gonna love all the things I bought!" she says, hugging him.

"I missed you, baby," Hurley whispers into her hair. Over her shoulder he sees a suspicious looking lump beneath the covers on her side. "I just can't do nothing when you're not here," he adds, returning her enthusiastic hug, wondering how he can get to that side of the bed first and make sure that Brandi did not leave panties or more between the sheets.

"Oh, Hurley, don't lay it on so thick!"

"No kiddin' baby, this house is a mausoleum with you gone. It needs your spirit to feel like a home. I just sometimes don't think I could live without you!"

"Why Hurley Brown," she says as if surprised. "You feel plenty alive to me. That boner of yours feels like you came home early with more in mind than just a pity fuck for your old girl."

That's it boy, Hurley thinks, *take one for the team!* Thinking about the threat the red-headed lawyer raises about Tuttle, he winces and feels his member go flaccid.

CHAPTER EIGHTEEN:
The Other Judge

Lilly Pruser senses that something is wrong as the screen of her iPhone fills with messages. She coasts into the garage, leaving the engine idling with the garage door open to keep the air conditioning running. The children, passed out in their booster and car seat, can sleep a little longer as she checks her messages before the chaos of unloading begins. She turned the phone off at midnight to focus on the road. It's now five in the morning, and she has about a dozen missed calls, mostly from the Center.

She left Missouri the afternoon before. Bobby and Lauren are five and three, so it is just so much easier to make the drive at night when they are sleeping. She loves being on the road and is a great late-night driver. She uses the time to think. To plan events. To daydream about conversations she wished she'd had rather than the ones she had.

"What's up, Felipe?"

"Are you home?"

"Yes, just got in. Waiting for the housekeeper to come outside before I try to unload the kids. We drove all night but they're still sleeping."

"Get some sleep and come in as soon as you can," he tells her and fills her in on what happened during the night.

"How is Judge Baker?" she asks.

"Still in surgery and we don't know. But it sure didn't look good."

CHAPTER NINETEEN:
The Brain

Finally, we sleep!

Deservedly.

They sewed him up pretty well, I'd say.

His breathing comes regularly.

I am tired. This has been a long night and morning, and I am tempt-ed to shut down myself for a little bit and just recalculate where we are.

But I can't do that. As I go through all these connections that have been broken it is so much easier to just reattach or reconnect them to each other as I find them and to observe the result, and then go to the next one when I get one to work right.

I guess we're a team in that regard, the doc and I...

As long as my man is restful, I work at a reasonable pace so as not to disturb him.

We are still on ice anyway.

Some of my systems don't seem to have gotten sewed back in where I would have done it, but it is easy enough for me to readjust their connections as we rest.

Let's face it: this doc is good. But he's human.

I know I helped him get this far and we are at least alive.

My man stirs again and tries to move.

Why can't he go with the flow ... but I stop myself. This is what we want from him! To see what's left in there.

Show me how you are, I say. Think away, I tell Judd, and as a re-ward I bring him his favorite moment. He never tires of that grandson.

I watch the memory unfurl into his consciousness without a single hang up.

Thank God, I say, just as little Tripp looks at Judd and says:

"Grandpa, do fish go to heaven when they die?"

Judd Baker always hesitates before answering this question. His first thought is to say there is no actual heaven but that never comes out with this grandchild who he considers the best proof he's ever seen of a loving God.

Judd thinks a while and then turns to his grandson. "If I were God, yes I believe these lovely creatures would be welcome in my heaven."

The child laughs as if he has tricked the old man!

Mom said you would know better than she did cause you're the judge! He literally screams it and it echoes in Judd's mind.

"Something's going on in there," a sweet voice says and Judd does not know where it comes from, but whispers:

"Girl, if you don't like my peaches, don't shake my tree!"[1] She laughs as if she hears him; and I want to applaud. Because they did hear him, as did I!

Keep him out, a strong voice orders!

"Calm down," the sweet voice says. "You've got a long way to go. A no nonsense feminine voice. Another bossy woman to keep him straight!

---

[1]Another Willie Special from Austin Live

CHAPTER TWENTY:
The REAL Lawyer

"You're new here, aren't you?" Hurley smiles benevolently at the newspaper reporter, a pretty twenty-something woman. She is holding what he takes to be a copy of his lawsuit, filed that day on behalf of her employer and its star reporter. "They send you down to get the scoop?"

"Something like that," she says, sitting as if poised to write his words of wisdom into a notebook she balances on a crossed knee.

Nice legs, he thinks. "That's good," he says, smiling at the young reporter. "Little needs to stay away from it for now."

"They won't keep him out," she says, catching his smile with her own. "He'll still be writing, but it'll be on the editorial page where he can say, as usual, what he really has in mind to say, irrespective of the truth."

Both laugh at this.

A smart girl I can take to, Hurley thinks.

"Twenty million big ones," the girl muses. "How serious is the chance Mickey's going to walk away from this even a millionaire?"

"You want to know whether to soften him up as a possible meal ticket?"

She leans back in the chair and casts a level eye in Hurley's direction, lids lowered.

"There ain't enough money in the whole state of Texas, honey."

Hurley laughs. "I know what you mean!"

"Give me a quote about likely success for the paper," she says.

"This is a case about protecting the public," Hurley says, turning on a familiar machine in his head. "Given the egregious treatment of this fine reporter, one of our community's finest, it is very likely that this court action will result in a significant jury verdict against the public entities who with regularity hire people who are not fit, and then fail to train and supervise them in a manner that protects the public. When a government employee acts with such callous disregard for the rights of others—especially our precious right of a free press, it is appropriate to address the wrong with a proper monetary award. Moreover, Mr. Little and I, and the *Enterprise,* will continue to press the authorities to bring criminal oppression charges against this employee."

"Now you're talking," she says, having script-printed every word he said in amazing shorthand. He takes note of the scribbles and says:

"Let's go have a drink."

"Maybe next time," she promises.

"You win some, you lose some," Hurley says.

The girl laughs and looks back over her shoulder at him as she walks away. The look and shrug say to him: *Not in this lifetime for you, either, buddy.*

And she goes on her way.

Hurley shrugs but starts off in the opposite direction as if planned.

CHAPTER TWENTY-ONE:
The Other Judge

"Where do these people come from?" Lilly asks, tossing the file onto the corner of her coordinator's desk. Susan wearily takes the file and shakes her head.

"And why do we get them all?" Susan replies. "Ever think about that? I think somebody in the clerk's office sniffs them out and sends us anything remotely controversial. Look at all these smelly cases," she sighs.

"We need to keep a bag of Alpo on hand for these dogs," Lilly says.

"Sarah Johnson versus Prudence Whipple. Is that for real? I thought a Whipple was a nun's hat?"

"That gal sure don't look like a nun!"

Both women laugh.

"Let me sign that commitment order before I go back out. You know, I don't trust a word Hurley Brown ever says," she confides to the coordinator.

Susan snickers. "That's probably wise."

"Will you call the other lawyer and see if she wants this child psyched as he's suggesting? And hold the order until you talk to her, if you will, Susan. He's just a bit too organized with all these sign-off signatures that look pretty much as if he signed them all. Doesn't pass the sniff test."

"Never does with Hurley," Susan offers, already looking for McLeod's telephone number in the system.

Back in the courtroom, Lilly watches as Mrs. Johnson approaches the bench hesitantly. She carries an obvious burden and Lilly wants to let her know that when one door closes, often, another opens and life is better. But she can't. This woman is past middle age but still looks strong enough to do battle against the woman who, although younger, gives Sarah Johnson a wide berth at the bench.

"What are we looking at today, ladies?" Lilly asks, scanning the original petition the woman filed *pro se*.[4]

"Well Judge," Johnson says. "I am asking for a restraining order against Miss Whipple, here."

"And the grounds?"

Whipple interrupts: "Judge, she doesn't have grounds, and I intend to file my own request for a restraining order against her." The younger woman flips her red hair over her shoulder with an ugly look at Johnson. There's no way that bright color came from anything other than a cheap box dye.

One of those, Lilly thinks and goes through the file.

"But you haven't filed any such claim or papers yet, right?" Lilly asks the younger woman.

"Not yet, Judge, I have to work for a living."

"What do you do?"

"I'm an executive secretary at Baines Kaplan Investment and, until he retired, I worked for her husband Regis Johnson."

"Why don't ya'll just tell me what I can do for you?" Lilly asks, raising her right hand and nodding for them to do the same thing and repeating in rote fashion, looking at both in turn: "Do each of you solemnly swear or affirm that in the testimony you are about to give in this hearing, you will tell the truth, the whole truth, and nothing but the truth, so help you God?"

"I do, Judge, but I had to take time off to come down here and wait all morning because of this insane woman."

"Mrs. Johnson, what is it exactly that you are trying to do here?"

Johnson scowls. "Make her keep my husband, now that he's old and worn out. She spent a bunch of time and effort taking him away from me and now she wants to send him back because he sometimes

---

4   *Pro se* means that the litigant acts on her own behalf. Any citizen can appear pro se for himself as long as competent and making reasonable efforts to be rational in the papers filed, called pleadings.

wanders off and can't remember who he is and where he really lives. I want you to restrain her from putting him out on the streets alone, driving off, and leaving him."

"They are still married, Your Honor," Prudence Whipple says, rolling her eyes as if to let the judge know that she understands how stupid she finds this entire proceeding.

"And where does *he* want to go?" Lilly asks.

"That's just it. He doesn't rightly say much anymore, Judge," Mrs. Johnson explains. "He kinda forgets where he's supposed to be and then can't remember where he is and then he can't remember which one of us he's really married to. I'm just asking you to order her not to put him out on a strange street corner like she did last time. She shouldn't be allowed to kick him out of her car the way she did when she left him stranded at a café, because he really can't figure out anymore how to get home. If she would bring him back home or leave him at home in the first place, I hired a caretaker. But she picks him up like it's old times because his CPA still authorizes payment of some of her bills. But if he's not functioning the way she wants that day, she dumps him by the side of the road."

"Who is giving this CPA authority to do all that? Lilly asks and looks at Prudence, who has one hip cocked with a hand propped on it, her head tilted defiantly. *If she swishes that hair one more time,* Lilly thinks, *I am going to hold her in contempt and send her to jail for a month.*

"He's not my husband," Whipple says, "but we have a contract. He specifically is not my responsibility, but we agreed on what he pays a long time ago!"

"Then the wife's request seems reasonable *under those circumstances*," Lilly says. "You do concede the relationship?"

The younger woman nods.

"Is this something the two of you can work out if I send you to the jury room?" she asks.

"I'm not going into any jury room with her," the younger woman insists. "I'm afraid of her, Judge."

"Do you carry, Mrs. Johnson?" Lilly asks.

"I have a .45 but I didn't bring it to court."

Lilly looks across the courtroom where Ishmael Pope, the substitute bailiff, looks back up and meets her eye. She sees a twinkle.

Ishmael's thinking is transparent: *"Justice is mine, saith the Court!"*

"She went through the machine, Your Honor," Ishmael says, standing. "She has a license to carry. They checked her purse and the box with her papers in it. She doesn't have a gun with her. I could sit with them, Your Honor, if you want me to." A role he has played often in other cases.

"There, thank you. Sheriff Ishmael Pope is going with you ladies. Give them a time limit, Sheriff, and bring them back out here if they don't play nice. Counsel, I am going to take a quick break with your permission, then I'll be back."

She closes the door between the courtroom and her chambers.

"Susan, did we have two full moons this month? The whole world is going crazy."

Conspicuously, in the center of her desk, the coordinator has lined up the most recent edition of the *Enterprise* folded so that the front center story is apparent.

"Who is this Cleopatra Jones?" Lilly calls out.

The coordinator walks into chambers. "Never heard of her. You are going to get burned on this."

"Why should I get burned? It's not my doing. I was 600 miles away and driving 8 hours to get here when this all went down."

"That's part of the problem. Dickless says you were AWOL. He says you should have been here. Good judges man their court first, no matter who's sick. It's your court."

"It's the people's court. Felipe's a good employee and I intend to stand by him. Besides, there's no doubt he was in the right. The medics say he saved Judge Baker's life. He's a real hero."

"For sure," Susan says. "But you're up for re-election and seeking a promotion to District Court. You better hope this dies down quick."

"I can't worry about that now. What's this next case?"

"Old Wentworth dispute over land on the West End."

"*The* Wentworths?"

"Grandson. I think. Maybe not. May be trading on the name since he's black. Says he's been running adverse possession through his grandfather to reclaim something."

"Phony?"

"Probably. But...I don't think you ought to say so."

"I'll try to be a good girl since I'm up for re-election soon," Lilly says sweetly and Susan smiles.

"Did Shadow McLeod approve the request to psych that kid?"

"She's in court; I called but she was doing a plea. She's supposed to call us or come by."

"Let me know when you hear back from her." With that, Lilly heads back out into the fray.

"Collins versus Wentworth," Lilly calls, once back on the bench. "Come on up. What can we do for you today?"

"Well, young lady, this here's Bud Wentworth, the grandson of the old man Willie Wentworth, and he's trying to take some land his grandpappy sold to me for good cash money in the fifties, just before he died. He give me this deed and everythin' and sent me down to this courthouse to register it. And I filed it just the way he tol' me to. Yes, Sir. I mean Ma'am."

"Why don't you let him talk to me for himself and you tell me your part of the story first, Mr. Collins. Come on up here, Mr. Wentworth."

She puts them both under oath as she did the two women. As soon as they finish swearing, Mr. Collins starts again.

"Okay, Judge. Don't seem right, you know, talking to a woman up there."

"It's been a while since you've been to court, has it, sir?"

"Pretty much when I filed this deed was the last time I wuz here. 'Cept to vote."

"Well things change, but not so much with the law of property. This deed says Mr. W. W. Wentworth deeded you ten acres out of a 1,200-hundred-acre track on the West End of the Island."

"Way out," Collins says. "Almost to the pass."

"You paid all the taxes."

"Sure have."

"You lived there ever since you filed this deed?"

"Yes, Ma'am."

"Built a house?"

"Moved a trailer on it, Ma'am. Thirty foot double wide. Put in a

garden. That wuz how I come to know he is inching away at my property. Put his fence right on it, three feet into into my land.'"

"Mr. Wentworth, how did you run adverse possession against
land deeded to him by your…grandfather, was it?"

"Yes, Your Honor. My grandfather deeded ten acres to Mr. Collins, but my grandfather put up a fence to make the boundary so
Ray here would know where to stop mowing. Now, he says, and the
surveys show it too, that grandfather encroached on it and when I
replaced the barbed wire fence with a nice tall cedar one so I could
fence my pool, Mr. Collins shows up after the fact and says you got
your fence three feet inside my property."

"Let me see if I understand this," Lilly says, taking the aerial
photograph little Willie Wentworth is holding out. "Are these your
granddaddy's markings?"

"Yes Ma'am, I expect so."

"How long ago do you think he made these marks?"

"It was in the fifties for sure," Collins cuts in. "That's the same plat
he handed over to me. That one right there under your thumb is where
his daughter built her house. Some people call it a mansion and it's big,
but it ain't uppity-looking like this here young'uns puttin' in."

"When was her house built?"

"About two years before I put my trailer down," Collins says.
"That's what the reason was he wanted to mark my property off and
took me to the courthouse to file it as a protection, to make sure nobody else could claim it."

Wentworth says, "Judge, isn't there a rule against quoting dead
men?"

"I'll take that as an objection and sustain it. Mr. Collins, without
telling me what Mr. Wentworth said to you, tell me what your understanding of these other markings are."

The old man looks the document over closely and hands it back
to the judge.

"That one under your finger belonged to his daddy," he says, motioning toward the grandson. "He's the one that kilt himself drinking
too much. This here boy is like' him in some respect, 'cept he don't
drink, he smokes that mary-ju-anna."

The young man squirms.

"I'm going to disregard all of that as irrelevant. Just tell me about the land."

"Well, when he ain't high, he and I get along just fine, but he must'a laid this fence of his when he was high. It's crooked and it cuts in three feet or more right here." He points to a definite curve in the line of the fence, and a long triangle of land along the fence. "Now, he don't want to change the line cause he says it'll costs too much money to take the fence down."

"Well, I think that fence was put there by my grandfather, and if it was, the problem was with him," the younger man says.

"Hold on, was this fence not put up by the grandfather?" the judge asks for clarification.

"No ma'am, my grandfather just put up a barbed wire fence. Collins says my grandfather's fence was there," he pointed to a spot on the image, "but his fence was crooked too, I just followed the fence line that was already there."

"But Judge, that ain't true. I mowed that land all these years and the old barbwire was never crooked."

"What about his mowing claims?" she asks the younger man.

"I'm not saying he didn't mow it, at least when my grandfather was alive."

"Anything else?"

"No, Your Honor."

"I don't reckon, young lady."

"Well, if I look at the two of you, I think I have two credible people before me. To break the tie of equal credibility I'm giving both of you, I'm going to look at this plat his grandfather made for you, Collins, that was filed with the county, and compare it with the aerial photo of the current fence. It's hard to tell exactly where the fence line is on the old drawing. But if you'll look at the drawing and at the photo, Mr. Wentworth, you'll see that every other line is straight as an arrow, except for your fence. Your grandfather never drew a crooked line. Looking at your grandfather's plat, I have to rule for Mr. Collins and order you to take down that portion of your fence that encroaches on his land."

Wentworth frowns. Collins generously doesn't celebrate too obviously.

"Shake hands, gentlemen, and go home. You're gonna be neighbors for a long time."

Both men do so, and Lilly takes another break.

"Miss McLeod doesn't know anything about Hurley's order," Susan tells her when she again is in Chambers. "She says she's coming by to look at it because she didn't sign it. She doesn't object to the psych exam, but would like more client involvement in the decision. She's asking for time to go talk to the child."

"It's too late," Lilly says. "Didn't we let the kid out with a caretaker?"

"I thought so," Susan says. "But Miss McLeod doesn't think the psych exam will do any good if the child is not in agreement."

"I agree with her," Lilly tells the coordinator. "Tell her we'll hold the order until she calls you, but to get it done fast."

As Lilly starts back to the bench, Susan stops her: "Judge, I like the way you handled those Wentworth guys."

"Well, thank you, Susan."

"I just want you to know I'm on your team. I really hope you get that bench. If a man gets the position, he'll have it for life. I know Fee Lo's rooting for you, too."

"Well, thank you Susan." Lilly says.

"Now go lay down the law on that Prudence woman!"

"Ugh, do I have to?"

Both laugh as Lilly pretends to drag her heels leaving the judge's chambers. She loves her job, even if sometimes cases like the one that's up make her lose a little faith in humanity.

CHAPTER TWENTY-TWO:
The Deputy

"Felipe!"

The voice calling his name reminds him of his mother's, the specific tone she used when he was in trouble growing up. Lilly Pruser might be younger than his mother, but he can't escape the authority in her voice. While most of his coworkers call him Fee Lo, Lilly always uses his full name at work. He would consider them friends, but they keep a level of formality: he always calls her *judge*.

Today, there's a note in her voice that promises punishment, just like his mother's used to. He takes a deep breath, thinking, *here it comes!*

"Yes, Judge."

"When you get a minute."

"Sure, Judge. Can I take this fella back to jail first? I don't have anything to cuff him to and I need to get him there in time for lunch."

"I have to leave for the Juvenile Board Meeting at 3."

"I can make it. If not, can we talk tomorrow?"

"Sure, when it's convenient."

Part II

CHAPTER TWENTY-THREE:
Home of the Hardy and Brave

This Hurley dude is getting under my skin.

When the court called me today to say I had signed a letter and a proposed order sending Phoebe to a lock-down, I finally realized that not only must I stay to challenge what this lawyer is doing, but I must insist that as far as she is concerned, I am her only lawyer. She professes to distrust Hurley, but I know and recognize there is a big possibility she is playing both of us. But he has a major conflict and can't ignore it under the rules of the Bar.

Her grandfather is apparently paying Hurley big bucks to represent Phoebe and Hurley wants to make sure that I do not interfere with his "sandbox," as he calls it. I have no desire to do that. I will take whatever I get when I'm paid by the county.

It has now been six weeks since Fee Lo called me to the Center to represent this young woman and I admit I feel bonded to her in a way I never expected to because I now know she's been put through a lot—some of it because she was naïve and didn't realize this dude was using her to draw in other girls he is also abusing—but most of it is what this dude's manipulation has led to. I feel I know what Phoebe's best defense is and, Hurley, if he stays in the case, will ensure that doesn't happen because, for whatever reason, he is saddled with Tuttle, maybe for life.

Hurley seems to be on a roll but is, for now, tolerating what he sees as *my* interference.

Although in the past I have walked away when caught in a situation like this where someone already has a lawyer when I am appointed, the difference here for me, is that Hurley represented Henry Ace Tuttle in the mess that led to Judge Baker's retirement. Now, given what I think is Tuttle's role as the drug supplier, for my young woman and others, Hurley will work to prevent my underaged client from raising her best defense. I am also beginning to believe that Tuttle's influence over Phoebe clearly rises to the level of human trafficking. At least one of the witnesses has given me a statement that Tuttle loaded both girls up on something before it happened. She described the victim as a nice kid, although she has no good words for Phoebe. She thinks Phoebe helps Tuttle to the point she will encourage younger girls to believe his vows of love for them.

We call it grooming where I come from.

I have told Hurley that nothing in the practice manuals say that I have to step aside, and since I am here by court order, I am staying. But his response is usually: "We'll see."

In fact, the judge has said she is keeping me on.

But I know enough to know that I am still considered a newcomer to this jurisdiction and that I don't know fully what leads Hurley to have such confidence in his position.

I do my usual.

I go first to the Rosenburg Library, thinking I will just take a look at anything I find that tells me more about this Hurley, who thinks he can put me out of business. I find only his mother's files as Mayor. She served for a decade and folks obviously loved her. She had a sense of humor and someone quoted her nearly every day.

I go to the *Enterprise* offices and ask permission to go to the morgue, a place in the newspaper's office that houses its archives. I guess it is called a morgue since old papers go there to die slow deaths. Some of the documents in this one have been around for longer than a century.

Susan Miller, the librarian, comes into her office and her face lights up, "What are we looking for today?"

"I think Hurley Brown, if you have anything on that gentleman."

"Well, for one thing," Susan says. "Hurley is no gentleman, but the whole town knows Hurley, so we probably have some stuff on him. What's he up to now?"

"He's telling me to get off a case the judge appointed me to. I just want to know where he gets off making such instructions to people."

"Well, that is like you to want to know who you're fighting before you fight."

We both smile. It is true. "And I love this particular kind of library,"
I say. "My first job before I even got out of college was filing in the
morgue for the local papers. I thought I could get my foot in the door as
a writer. That didn't work, but it did convince me to go to law school."

"I'll bet you're happy about that," she says.

"Some days," I concede. "Let's see what you have on him."

This Susan reminds me of the Susan Brown who works for Lilly
Pruser, since both seem to be in total control of their environment and
they are *no nonsense women.* This Susan loves selling her library to
newcomers. "It may be better if you look at just a few of the history files
first since they will tell you who had influence and if you have to worry
about Hurley, you'll see the reason he's wearing on most people."

She brings me files and are they ever full.

"Obviously there's a lot I don't know and haven't heard of," I say
with a laugh.

"Some of Texas' brightest and boldest are in these files," Susan
says, handing me a faded clipped article.

"You might want to look at this first. Townsend wrote it in his
early days."

I have met Jim Townsend now three times and know he came to
the *Enterprise* when two of his mentors in Dallas got him out of town
after he pissed off their publisher. He has been here ever since and
started as a rookie reporter.

I read his by-lined story about snake island:

> *Many moons before this story, a lonely rattlesnake
> climbed upon a log to sun and, lo and behold, the water
> surged beneath him as the tide came in and rolled the poor
> snake out to sea.*
>
> *He would have tried holding tightly to the log but it was
> so large, and he had no hands. He could only wrap himself
> about it once.*
>
> *The log floated along long enough for the snake to begin
> to feel the strong effects of a battering sun and heat and the
> knowing feeling that he had absorbed and processed that
> last jumping thing with long ears and that perhaps he was
> past due for another. Fortunately for him, the log hit the
> dirt and in the hands of a burly wave, was cast upon a coast*

after flaying itself end to end in the broken surf. Ultimately,
the rattlesnake catapulted in a long serpentine spiral from
the log into the sand.

It was not bad. These new surroundings were full of
weathered live oaks, cedars only man tall, salt marshes,
and humidity[5]. But the sand was too hot for his belly that
slid across the surface of it, so he dug in, remembering that
world from before whence he came. He found that cooler
layer of ground where he could snuggle in and digest things
after finding suitable prey. The grasses grew tall around him
and lots of long ears and no ears, ducks, herons, and deer[6]
waited without any hint of fear of him. Edibles all, they
largely laid around for his taking.

He easily filled himself on a laughing gull that had seen
better days. As such things go, over time, the rattler became
aware he had left interesting things behind when the log
on which he had been sunning set out to sea. He began to
watch the waves and even birds that flew over, hoping he
would catch a glimpse of what it was that he was missing.
But since like most animals, he lived very much in the present tense, he had to wait until he saw it to know what it is
that was missing.

And it happened.

She fell from the sky after her venom took its effect
on the pelican that had tucked her inside its scandalously
large beak. Not much was said, but the attraction of these
two was immediate and created an entire new ecology for
this lonely atoll. Before long there were little ones, and the
lovely land was no longer attractive to any passing ship.
Sailors no longer stopped here in search of fresh water or
local fruits, because sailors spread the word that this atoll
was now identified on their maps and memories as *Snake
Island*. It was covered with such creatures.

---

5   David G. McComb, *History of Galveston, A History and a Guide.*
See Introduction 1-4, He missed entirely the arrival of the snake; but described
the flora and fauna as set out here but for the weight of the humidity; but
Galveston's heavy air is famous for its weight.
6   Id. at 6.

Land being what it is and sparse even along the edge
of these vast waters, ships came by and it appeared their
number was increasing all around Snake Island. But Snake
Island was largely left to the creatures who crawled on their
bellies until the inevitable arrival of the two-legged creatures who never did a blasted thing that benefited the environment anywhere they walked.

~

"This isn't complete, Susan." I hand it to her. "For me, lethargy
takes over as soon as I get to the bridge. I think it's the humidity. How
can that possibly lead to sin and corruption, because that's the other
thing people say about our lovely town."

"That is the funny thing about us," Susan says. "'Sin,' they say,
'has a way of sticking around when all else flees!' But our beaches
have been a tourist attraction since that snake landed accidentally.
His offspring fill the dunes, however paltry ours are considered to be.

"All the greats came through here. Here and New Orleans, which
also had a reputation for sin and corruption. Maybe it was the fact the
sea lures you and it makes you feel sexy," Susan says and laughs her
little girl laugh.

The remainder has been separated from the first paragraphs and
I put it aside, intending to ask for it back. "He had it last, reworking
it, I think," she says. Townsend is now the Senior Managing Editor of
the *Enterprise* and must have worked out his writer frustration after
that article because I see nothing else by him.

"A lot seems to have been written about Snake Island," I tell Susan. "That must mean part of it is true."

She laughs and hands me the next folder, which contains a similar
collection of Galveston stories by the reporter folks called The Babe,
because she was a cute little female reporter that Fee Lo is quite taken
with. She scares abusers of the system and has a long-running battle
with Rutter Industries. The Babe has instinct; she has nerve. When
she cannot get what she wants, she finds some guy who will get it for
her. Altogether she is a highly respected reporter and holds the Head-
liner's Award, Texas' highest journalistic award.

The next folder is about a woman I do not know that much
about but will if I read all of these articles. Jane Herbert Wilkinson
Long should be called the mother of Texas. She stood down dancing
Karankawa natives who allegedly intended to eat her—Shadow re-

membered—and bravely manned a fort with only her daughter, her slave girl, and the baby she was carrying.

"She says she did it alone," Susan says, "she claimed she even negotiated for her freedom with Jean LaFitte, the pirate and all-round-bad-boy of the era."

Jane ended up owning and operating a boarding house in Richmond, a short distance to the North and West of Galveston.

She was courted by the famous men of the era, Sam Houston, Mirabeau Lamar, Dr. James Long, who was her husband. A biography of Jane is featured on the online publication of the Texas State Historical Association.[7] Susan hands off a very old file in my direction. I take it and it feels like blowing dust is coming up off it.

"Oh, I love that," I say. "One reason I like morgues is because they do seem dusty and filled with ghosts. This one is old!"

"These are my favorite two women for different reasons," Susan says. "Neither got credit for their greatness! And both deserve it for different reasons. Jane Long may have been a very modern woman who, truthfully, liked variety in her men. She was courted by all but accepted none of them. After Dr. James Long abandoned her and got himself killed, I'll bet no man could have convinced Jane to ever marry again."

"Mary Moody Northern was a pretty girl who became an exceptionally sweet-looking older woman and she did something women generally were not allowed to do then. Her daddy left a big foundation with her for her to manage. She was a philanthropist who married and stayed married, but also ran a foundation and handled money—some $425 million—in a very responsible way.

"All things considered, Galveston is a special place. It was founded in the 1830s by land speculators, was developed by these entrepreneurs into the largest Texas City and largest deepwater port for the State until the City of Houston and the Port of Houston seized those honors.

"Mary Moody," Susan says, "Set aside some funds to create an honor for Jane as the mother of Texas, but it was not to be. They hired Paul Green, a well-known playwright who specialized in historical plays, the outdoor theater productions of the time to do a play about Jane's adventure but Green decided that people didn't want to see feisty

---

7   This organization may be visited on line at https://tshaonline.org. handbook/online/articles/flo11.

women in a play but devoted his play to buck-skin wearing Texas men such as Sam Houston and others to create mock war skirmishes and fire off long guns and cannons. The play and the theater were a hit, despite the fact the theatre was surrounded by man-eating mosquitos and other nightlife. People ran as soon as the mosquitos descended on them.

Green could find no real evidence to show that Sam Houston had ever been here for anything other than two short episodes in which Sam probably tried to convince a prissy Methodist preacher that Galveston was NOT a sin city. The preacher got sick and took to his bed, sick. Most likely, Sam's idea of sin was far different from the Right Reverend Littleton Fowler.

Sam came again and tried to convince Galvestonians to stay with the Union during the Civil War and almost got run out of town on a rail.

That quick exodus also was necessary for the weatherman Isaac M. Cline in 1900 who said for people to work til noon and then go home and by noon, there was no city left and no homes for people to go to.

"Those were dark days," Jim Townsend says, joining Susan and me for coffee which he is delivering himself. He has three coffee machine disposable cups balanced on the thick file.

We thank him profusely, but he returns my grin and asks me why I suddenly got so interested in Galveston history.

"I have a problem."

"You can share," he replies.

"Off the record?"

"Unless I already have it."

"That's a deal," I say. "One of your locals is trying to fire me from a job I took on the other night for a Juvenile facing very serious charges. He says I have to bow out, but I don't think I'm going to. I just came to see if there is a reason he dictates terms to the rest of us."

"The gentleman giving you trouble has no good reason to think he is empowered to hand down those orders to the rest of us. You shouldn't step aside," Townsend says. "I know that case. It's about time that young girl had a lawyer looking out for her and not himself. Stay in there and fight. I'll back you up if the time comes."

I always thought Jim Townsend knew his town better than most editors; but that convinces me.

I look at Susan and wink. I loved being with her and going through those dull, boring old files about the people who provided the foundation for this small town that I'm beginning to think of as home!

CHAPTER TWENTY-FOUR:
Shadow

I toss my file on the desk that my mother bought me to give me courage, and sink into my fire engine red leather executive desk chair. I want to cry, but I won't. Sometimes I feel this chair and desk have more gumption than I do.

I shake my head, trying to clear it by erasing the last three hours in District court Number 213 in Galveston County, Texas.

Take your choice on any day—when it is for or against me, the law they govern by here seems alien sometimes!

"I feel a hissy fit coming on," my legal assistant calls out from the back where she is making copies for discovery. "What happened?"

"The usual, but I will find a way to work around that judge's ruling! Science alone should show the error. I just am so tired of being treated like a New Yorker who should have stayed in her own town and keep her opinions where people are not real humans anyway. I just feel like a red-headed stepchild who can't get a fucking ruling in her favor anywhere in this town."

"Well, that is probably not true," Phyll says. "You come back with your own cache of good rulings that I can't believe sometimes. And, you, of all people, are very good at finding a way around any roadblock. *You always pull it out*, as your friend Fee Lo says."

"Yes," I say. "I'm just mad at me. Deep down I did not think that anybody living in the twenty-first century could make such a crazy ruling and not be embarrassed. But he wasn't. All I had to do was persuade a crazy man not to act crazy."

"What did happen?" Phyll asks again.

"Just exactly what I knew would happen." I say.

"It's okay because you recognized it was a long shot."

"Yes, but it was a long shot that was the right shot."

"Maybe she was too well known on the waterfront," Phyll suggests, which I had also considered.

"She didn't try to hide that. Virgins seldom get charged with soliciting anyway," I say. "She has proved herself to be a good mother, who takes excellent care to find good childcare for the baby when she is working, same as many other women. But this judge did not buy my argument on her behalf and did not give her the time of day, much less $50 in child support—which is nothing, far less than the statute puts out for the unemployed. And this old guy makes pretty good money."

"We are just going to have to figure out a plan that he can't ignore," Phyll says. "First, you knew in advance that we do not have soliciting on the island. And second, even if we did, married men have no reason to seek out services from ladies of the evening and you know in your heart that they don't."

"Sure," I say. "I know, you predicted that," I say, "and that was the deciding factor here. The 'putative father,' the judge told me, flatly and clearly, is a married man and thus could not have fathered a child with a prostitute."

"See," Phyll says. "The judge's scientific understanding is impeccable!"

"I'll figure out something."

"I know you will, girl. You always do!" she agrees. "Your buddy just drove up in that noise machine," Phyllis says. "He will make you feel better about things."

"Okay, I'll bite. What is this?"

I look at the list that she hands me as she nods for Fee Lo to come on back. "The coast is clear," she tells him.

Her note has five people identified as youths and five as adults.

"What is this now?" I ask again.

"This is the beginning of your new support group."

"Okay," Fee Lo, says "And when do I get this support?"

Fee Lo is holding out his hands as he walks into the room.

"I guess you're the friend?" Phyllis asks.

"I would go ahead and call both of you douchebags," Fee Lo

says, mostly to shock Phyll. "But a pair like you wouldn't take offense, would you," he sneers.

"No more than you would if I told the world your rubber keeps
falling off," I figure that is the way their friendship will go because
he gives Phyll a good laugh as well as applause.

"This is my good friend, Fee Lo," I tell Phyll. "You can see the
kind of man I attract."

I stand and he crosses the room and we hug as we always do. We
hug each other for just a moment too long.

"That's nice," Phyll says, her voice so flat it slides out. I met her
during an unfortunate episode with my first husband, and Phyll has
openly crusaded to find me a man who meets her demands for me. She
mostly never meets a man she thinks is eligible for me that she dislikes,
but, I sense one coming on here from the looks she gives Fee Lo.

"That's nice," I say to Fee Lo, hugging him again and repeating
her words and the almost silent *humph* and attempt to leave.

"Do you want the door closed?" she asks.

"No," I tell her. "I may need your help. But tell me, please, how is
this support going to work? Tell me before you leave because I know
you will know what to do with it and I'm not sure I do."

"The class wants to help. "

"That's great," I say and I mean it. "Maybe they can start with
Phoebe, but I need to meet with them so that it will be clear what we
can and cannot do and it is important for me to know what they are
planning to do."

"I'll set it up," she says and again she tries to leave, succeeds, and
closes the door. I hear the machine start up again. Phyll has no equal
when it comes to paralegal work, even if it is copying depositions.

❧

I turn back to Fee Lo. "I swear," I say. "You always have the
smell of your last woman hovering about you, Fee Lo. Always. Or do
you use a feminine after shave?"

He looks at me like I am evil.

"You speak with a fork-ed tongue, tall woman."

"Me and the Devil," I agree. I'll bet you have heard that all your
life. What's up?"

"The rent and a place to stay. I've sublet my loft this afternoon till this is over. I need one of those rooms upstairs and I will not bring a woman to it unless she tells me it's a come-on and then I will be forced to."

"So you can't pay the rent. What happened?"

"My brave-hearted woman fired me this morning. Well, she didn't fire me, she put me on formal leave pending an investigation; but I had to clean out my desk, which means for all practical purposes, I'm not going back and at the end of the month, my pay will stop. So I'm fired."

I rise from my power chair.

"Bullshi-it," I say, drawing it out. "She's not involved in the firing mess, is she?"

"Nope. She stayed out of that. But she's running this year to move up to a district bench. I understand. She's got enough problems. If she fails to grab this new bench while it's open, it will go to a white male and that's where it will stay with somebody else and she'll never get it. These are crazy fucking times!"

"Crazy, my ass," I say, sounding more like him than me. "Dickless Little is wrong on this. She, of all people, should see that."

"She needs a quick out," he says. "Dickless doesn't want her to be a District Judge. She wears a skirt to work and she employs this guy who violated the First Amendment under color of state law! He's got a real enemy this time."

"I know. I fear I am reading between the lines to make it all right. You bastard. You hater of the Constitution. You ought to be fired."

"Thank you, Mrs. Lincoln. Now, let's go to the theater and complete the job!"

We both laugh although I feel more like crying.

"How can one person get away with what Dickless Little routinely does by crying freedom of the press. He sets up his own emergency. I read that story. There is nothing wrong with what you did."

"You know what's happening now. People believe what they want to believe. You can tell them a big whopper of a lie and they'll take it as true, I think, because it's better than boredom. These are just weird times.

"He sued me for twenty million big ones. I've got forty cents in my pocket," he says pulling out change. "Nope, make that thirty cents."

"He can't sue you! You acted in good faith; he could have been your perpetrator given his history with Judge Baker. And the arrest was no arrest: You held him as a material witness and even that was based on reasonable probable cause. I was there that night. Remember? I heard it straight from you. Everything you did. I told you it was okay if it proved to be witness protection you were doing. What the f—, sorry I know you don't like for women to use that word."

"Not *real* women. You're different. That learned legal giant Dickless Little says I stripped him of all constitutional rights and threw him to the dogs. I hate that bastard, Shadow. I've said so many bad things about him, nobody is gonna have trouble coming up with something I've said about Dickless Little to show how much I hate him!"

He does hate that reporter, I think that I would have to admit if asked in Court.

"Hell, I have so much malice in my heart toward him I go out of my way to get in his face whenever he shows up! This time, I just happened to be right."

"You don't have actual *malice toward him in your heart,*" I say, murmuring behind my hand, "even if you do *hate* him on a personal level, that *actual malice* would make you liable—"

"He sued her too, though. Seventy-five million from her for failure to supervise me and failure to realize I was a poor fucking bastard from the Valley, who had it in for God-fearing people everywhere else, especially his minions in the press!"

"It's called throwing you under the bus, Fee Lo!"

"She did tell me she let the county know that it might be helpful if they worked an early settlement against me, since he doesn't have a prayer of a chance of getting money out of her. She has judicial immunity."

"Do you realize how low that is?"

"Nah, she doesn't mean it that way; she is just shaken up and she thinks he will go away if he gets a little money and has bragging rights. I told her it would be okay if she has to do that to settle things down. I feel like I let her down. I know how to fly under the radar; I just lost it when I saw him taking pictures of the Judge upside down in muddy water and that bastard did nothing to even lift his face out. I should have arrested him for a crime against humanity!"

"Don't let it bother you that much. You'll win ultimately. Sad that she wants that job that badly," I say.

"She doesn't have a choice. She's got two kids to feed and she's getting rid of her old man, who is worthless in all respects. And she's about to lose her mother. I just feel sorry for her. She trusted me to keep out of trouble and I've let her down."

"I hope the angels that guard us read this right," I say. "I understand what you're saying and I even appreciate your loyalty even if you don't believe in good and bad angels who watch over us; but she should not want that bench that badly."

"Maybe not" he says. "I like women for reasons other than what most folks think. I like that too but I do know how hard it is to be a woman in this world. You don't get a fair break."

"At heart, you're a chauvinist."

"No I'm not and you know it. I'm a chauvinist with you because I want you and you're not having any of that."

"And Phyll?"

"Phyll would cut my dick off if I touched her. I know you two douchebags."

"No, I say. We love you. We both have a sister complex over you."

"Then you won't mind representing me," he says. "I do feel abandoned by the powers that be and I am looking for another lawyer for the county to pay, if good time-records are kept," he says, handing me a stack of papers. The one on the top causes me to automatically calculate the answer date.

"Phyll will shit bricks when you tell her we are taking this," he says as if he has already become one of our team. "I'll help," he says; "I have a plan."

"You want me to do this?" I ask him, holding the papers out as if he is to take them back. "The red-headed stepchild of the county. Why guarantee a loss like that?"

"We are not gonna lose," Fee Lo promises. "I have a plan that is sure to work if I'm right. But I need time. All I want you to do is to write the county a letter saying you represent me since they are abandoning me, and that if they settle my case before I have a chance to defend myself, I am going to sue each and every one of them for not defending me! And, tell them they have to pay your ridiculously high attorney's fees because I don't have any money now that they have frozen my pay, and you probably still need to pay your rent. That is for real—they will pay your fees so tell Phyll to keep good time records."

"You tell her; she'll like you more for it. What else am I going to do?" I ask cavalierly. "Deputy Fee-leap-ay Ur-r-r-rh-nan-dez." I toss my head a couple times and accent his name with as good an Hispanic trill of the r-r-r-r-s as I can command.

He laughs. I join him good-naturedly, but I am also worried for him because he has no walking around money most of the time.

"What will you do?"

"I've got my bullet-proof reflector vest and my personal handgun and my bike. I'll direct traffic for arenas and shopping malls, and trucks carrying those oversized loads, and I'll empty out my buildings before I let any other person on the road. What is the worst thing that could happen?" he asks.

"You'll never work again?" I ask.

"I just told you. I've got a plan. I'll start my own Black-Hawk—call it Crazy Chicano Hawk—you've said I can live in one of those little bitty rooms upstairs…"

"Well, that's sure a plan for living in splendor," I say. "Your women are really going to be impressed. At least you are keeping your sense of humor!"

"Yes. Do you still have that piece of shit car? Specifically, the one with five wheels and a garden chair held up by twine."

"Where would it have gone?" I ask. "Of course, it is the only car I have."

"Can I borrow it?"

"And am I going to rely on public bus service again to get me around town and to and from the West End?" I say. "Like last time when you gave me a schedule for buses that don't run."

"I'll get you a loaner from somebody. Or you could take my Harley."

"I'll think about that one," I say. "I can already see the bailiffs hanging out the window making catcalls when I come up in my Catwoman Motorcycle Ensemble."

Deep inside, it doesn't bother me to think about driving that bike.

"Where I'm going, I need to not make a statement with the Harley, and I promised my Mama I wouldn't drive it anymore on the highways. So I can't go home with it."

"Ah-hah," I say. "So there is one woman you let boss you around. Like you're not a cool dude who drives a Harley. I hear you coming two blocks away."

"I truly need not to stand out with what I'm planning."

"And you won't in the wretched wreck?"

"Not as much. Besides, I'll look poor."

"Well, that's true," I concede.

"With you it's still confidential. Right? Haven't we always been that way? I will give you another quarter when it won't leave me with just a nickel in my pocket. You're my attorney. I can tell you anything and you can't talk."

He actually did that once. In fact, on the day we met, he tried to scam me.

"Most anything," I say. "Sometimes I have to talk. Are you going to commit a crime?"

"Maybe, if it takes it."

"Is anybody in imminent danger of coming to physical harm at your hands?"

"Just you if you ever let me have my way with you."

"Yeah," I grunt. "Like I'm gonna get in line to roll over for love-'em and leave-'em pretty-happy Fee Lo Hernandez. Don't hold your breath."

He laughs again as I throw him the keys to the wretched wreck, my beloved 1963 Pontiac LeMans and he tosses the Harley key back to me. I tell him sternly:

"Don't bring it back empty; I just filled it up on my way back from getting the-you-know-what beat out of me. His excellency, Judge Poe, allowed B.J. Foster to wipe the floor with me on a child support case for a lady of the evening."

"Ladies of the evening are better off if they stay out of court," Fee Lo says. "Don't scratch up the bike. I'll gas the car up again when I bring it back. So there."

He blows me a kiss and then says:

"Seriously, I need to put some things upstairs if you are going to let me borrow one of those little bitty room. I've sublet my loft for six months. It may be on the market after that. And don't worry about my night life, women go apeshit sexy in those little rooms."

"Of course they do," I say.

Still laughing, he closes my door just as Phyllis breaks in.

"Don't tell me. He's taking your car again?"

"Just for a couple days," he tells her. "You like my Harley, I know. I talk to Justin. He tells me everything!"

He is still laughing as he closes the front door and heads away.

"Please don't take my car and leave me that motorcycle," She says almost pleadingly.

"Justin likes the Harley."

"Yeah, but my broad ass doesn't sit too well on it!"

"Your ass is no longer that broad, as you say, and you know what Justin says?"

"I know, I'm getting it ready for him. How long is your friend gonna be gone?"

"He didn't say. I didn't ask. Think of it more as a period in which you get extra lovin' and don't worry about it. You don't even have to comb your hair in the morning. You have a legitimate excuse for once."

I lean back and put in a CD I bought over the weekend at the Museum of Fine Arts, Houston, which offers them sometimes with an exhibit. It all goes together so well in that very creative period in Europe. It is a Degas Era piece of Rococo music from France and soothes as it flows from the Bose speakers, another gift from my mother. I try to let it lull me away from place and time as they promised. Away from the fucking courthouse and whatever Felipe Hernandez is up to.

Fee Lo and I fell together accidentally during a case in which, if I had been able to do so, I would have elevated that bastard judge in that case right out of the courtroom and into an abyss somewhere in a galaxy far, far away.

Fee Lo was the best thing to come from that episode. He showed me how friends support each other and in fact made it possible for me to move and to support myself here. He sent me work so I could break the ties with a family that was beginning to drag me down. I still love them and they are all the family I will ever have but I love the new life so much that I will stay, however crazy it might get at times.

His friendship keeps me going.

Maybe we never romanced because both of us left something important on that courtroom floor. The love of his life was exposed as having played him big time at the same time she was playing my brother or cousin, Bubba, the little boy who was built like a tank and was the collective bodyguard of every child at the Crow's Nest, and whether my brother or my cousin, whichever he is revealed to be, if they ever give us that insight, Bubba will be my protector. The Babe used him. I saw it happening . And when I met Fee Lo he was looking for her under the name The Babe. Bubba knew her under the name of Lorena. Each of them professed to me that this woman was the love of their life. I told both what I thought was happening. Fee Lo said he got the message but it is more than a couple years later now and he still carries that torch. Bubba is the same. The Babe has something— whatever it is!

And I had an abrupt epiphany about *who I am* as I stared Bobby Gene Simpson in the face, daring him not to answer my question. That revelation knocked both of my boot-clad shoes right out from under me. I still feel that blow at times because it is hard to stay grounded when everything in your life does a whoopsie doo like that, head over heels. My mother never told me who my father was and never let me make a decision on my own. But being a curious kid I went looking. I was wrong until it hit me and was as clear as day. It was Fee Lo who came to my rescue and I will never forget that.

CHAPTER TWENTY-FIVE:
Down In The Valley

Fee Lo gears the 1963 Pontiac LeMans down to help it make the crest of the last hill in the deep bottom of the Texas Hill Country before the environment settles into one long open plain, dotted by an occasional dying live oak, some sage, and a generous crop of huisache, *acacia farnesiano,* between San Antonio and Laredo. The rugged old plant is beautiful in the spring. Its yellow flowers float in the air like feathers when the wind blows through them and the essence from their stamens makes its way into perfumes and other scented oils.

His mother pointed all of that out to Fee Lo; although all his life she called him Little Feely because dad was Felipe and there could be only one of those. In fact, Evie's nickname grew out of mom's but Evie knew that Fee Lo would not tolerate her putting out the nickname *"Little Feely"* at his Courthouse. The name and the Hui-sache story are two of his clearest memories of her. When he was a young boy he knew the *"Little"* was a special designation. "They are like feathers, *Little* Feely," he can still hear her say. "Here, touch it and see how soft the edges are. They glimmer when the wind blows through them, Feely, and each tiny yellow flower is surrounded by these fragile fronds. See Feely, they catch the light and then give it back to us!"

She was right, of course, and how he appreciates their beauty now, but how he suffered to stand still for anything she wanted to say to him as a child. As an adult, he is ashamed of the way he refused to let her make him aware of the things that she loved.

The road is straight, divided, and filled with a minimal amount of rolling, which is that feeling when the car tries to draw itself into another lane from the unevenness resulting from poor quality of work that comes with contractor fraud, a common condition on Texas highways. In fact, Fee Lo thinks it feels better than the last time he took this highway home. But he was on his bike then, and Shadow's car is old and worn out but also heavier than the bike and that could be the difference.

But maybe the state's favorite entitlement groups, home builders and road contractors, are getting a conscience! He hopes so because he wants nothing to drag him down today.

He is on the open road, under a big Southwest Texas cloudless blue sky, and has a cause to work on!

He is also going home.

Home is magical, and it calls out to him only when he senses trouble in the life that he has made for himself. It would not be fair, he thinks, to say that he has turned his back on home. He and his childhood friend, Pedro, still pick up where they left off the last time they saw each other.

And he has now read everything that San Antonio woman-hollering-creek-writer wrote and it is making home even more desirable. He thinks he should find Sandra Cisneros and ask her about the part in all her writing that sticks to his brain. Where did she find the beauty in it all? It seems to him still that she loved Mexican clothes, people, cooking sites and the landscape of South Texas and its flower cactus and huisache.

Before he read her, he would have sworn that despite the physical beauty, there was no beauty to being an Hispanic growing up in South Texas.

He read her almost surreptitiously because he just felt evading her, after Shadow had her say about it, was a sell-out!

But Fee Lo thinks he has no story to tell.

He has no streets that he roamed along but for those Pedro took him down.

There was no old woman like Mrs. Roberts, who took him in like she did Pedro. And Fee Lo was most angry that he didn't need any of those things.

Fee Lo laughs at himself now because he was such a brat and so angry that he had nothing to complain about.

Maybe his size. They called him Little Feely because his Dad was Big Feely at the plant, but he made up for that by buffing out and getting strong.

But Little Feely could not even complain about that because he had real parents, both of whom worked and ran a tight ship.

He tried as hard as he could to reward them by becoming the neighborhood punk. He knew it. He thought it was cool and recognized his own rebellion spewing up inside him because he had nothing to complain about.

He criticized everybody for mistreating Mexicans while he went to bed full and satiated, with his own tv and x-box and any electronic that came on the scene, and a woman who picked up the clothes he consciously dropped where he took them off.

He remembers the hatred that he felt, especially for the Church, as he grew up around kids who ultimately took to the streets. It was easier to steal and hide away from the Church than to stay in line behind that fella who was giving nickels to prayer boys in exchange for what he made them say were pleasures for both of them. Fee Lo told the Padre he was a talker and would talk because that was just his nature, and it scared the old man off. And they knew his father was an executive at Rutter and would certainly take exception to the Padre having favors from his boy.

Still convinced there are some things he will not do, Fee Lo took Pedro's advice on others:

"Just do the thing you end up doing, but do it well!"

"If you be grateful to any woman who lets you go there, you get there more often." Pedro added. His advice was sage thinking and it worked. Fee Lo now knows that.

Fee Lo starts laughing to himself considering Pedro, who is still his best friend and Fee Lo's scrambled life and the characters who marched through it in such a short time. He lets the laughter spill over and fill up the entire cavity of the old worn-out piece of junk Shadow McLeod drives to remind herself of what a prick her first husband is, all so she won't make that same mistake again.

The car is all she insisted on taking.

Because he insisted, she owed the money on it, not him!

Her clothes because he couldn't get enough selling them.

She did not even keep a coffee pot, although God knows she can't survive without coffee. Hell, he would not live as poor as she does if he had the family she comes from.

Maybe that's why he likes her so much: She's a rebel, just like him!

She'll fight in court, even when she's not sure about the full extent of what she's fighting for.

But she won't fight dirty.

Fee Lo will.

Fee Lo will fight dirty as long as it takes.

God knows Fee Lo will fight dirty.

Still, even with that upbringing, he learned how to stay below the radar. Undetectable. If they don't know you are coming you stay ahead and out of trouble.

He considers his mission. What he intends to do to Dickless Little if he is right about him before this whole thing is over. Knows he has the power because he has a great memory.

He lost his control over his environment with Dickless.

He should have ignored him and let him be Dickless and pretend he was helpful.

But Fee Lo lost it.

Lost the ability to stay under the radar.

Thinks seeing the judge that way got to him.

Growing up with injustice all around him, Fee Lo knew better than to challenge Dickless. But he did and now he has to wear the consequences or come out ahead.

And he is as alive this morning as he has ever been, fifty miles or less away from home with the smell of his Mama's kitchen already flowing into the car like magic from mind and memory. He always feels just a little taller and more successful that he ever feels when he's away.

The smell of nature also filters into the open windows.

Because he broke away from them doesn't mean he doesn't appreciate the taste of coming back to them.

CHAPTER TWENTY-SIX:
Lillies Fading

Lilly pulls into the parking lot of the Rehabilitation Center.

Turns the key.

Turns the car back on immediately because the heat outside swamps it.

The flat roofed, single-story building is unimposing and there's no reason for her to be intimidated by it. She envisions Judd Baker lying in his hospital room, surrounded by machines that beep vital signs and lines that seep fluid into his body and out and into tubs below.

She holds her breath, thinking she can't breathe.

"Don't be such a goddamned evil, selfish, loathful bitch," she chides herself. *"This man needs you now. He's been there for you sure enough!"*

She'd gone to see him the first day. It was right after that horrible Phoebe MacPearson docket. Doctors were still hovering to see what was still alive; but one of Judd's doctors stops her and ushers her into and out of the room.

"I recognized you," he said, "And the Judge's daughter told me to make sure I tell you everything I tell her. HIPPA keeps me from telling either of you much. But his daughter told me to give you anything we can give her. She thinks you can help him, that you are the best he can get because he loves you and she knows that and she wants to keep her Daddy. But he's anybody's guess right now, and it depends on how much of a fighter he is."

"He's a fighter," she says. "He's not ready to check out. He'll make it."

They let her walk in briefly alone.

She touched his arm. At least his body is still warm.

She leans in close.

"I love you," she whispers but is not sure she means it for this shrunken, heavily bandaged, wasted-looking old man.

"I need you," she adds and hears the weakness in her own voice. That is true. She does need him and wants him to be the way he has always been.

And then the same doctor ushers her from the room.

How long did they let her have? She thinks.

A minute?

Two minutes?

Daily afterward, she calls or goes by and goes in. Sometimes she leaves in tears and can't drive until the crying passes.

Seeing him, unable to even sit it a chair without help is too much. He cannot yet stand, much less stand alone!

CHAPTER TWENTY-SEVEN:
Family Newspapers

Jim Townsend tallies up the advertising space needed for the morning edition and adds to it the column lines reported by the City Editor on must-runs and totals the number of pages to lay out for the next days' morning edition.

"You called," Mickey Little says from the doorway.

"Yeah, Mickey, come on in. Let me take a minute to send this over to Sue so she can lay out tomorrow's early run," he holds up his paper of scribbles and picks up the phone.

"I can come back," Little offers, a little peeved at having to wait.

"No, I need to talk to you." He motions Mickey in and to a chair but the Reporter remains standing by the door. "Sue, this is Jim. I'm emailing fourteen pages. Can you get it all in and do the breaks for separate sections."

He waits for a response, still motioning Mickey to come in.

"Okay try and call me back."

"Fourteen's a pretty good number," Mickey says.

"Good enough, we're turning a low profit these days."

"I like to think I am helpful in that area," Little says, not even trying to hide his hint for confirmation.

"Oh, you do your part, that's for sure, Mickey. You've got a good following. That's what I need to talk to you about. What is so stuck in your craw about Judd Baker?"

"Oh nothing really. He is just another self-centered dickless prick judge as far as I'm concerned."

"He's retired you know. Some people give you credit for that."

Little smiles.

"But a lot of people think he's an alright guy."

"No," Little says, a tinge of disgust in his voice. "They think he don't put on his pants like the rest of us. That name, some people think he walks on water. He just don't."

"Well, while he's going through this rehab stuff, he is a local hero, and he was shot down by a crazy person for doing his job. That's all he ever did. The job he had to do. That hearing that you and Hurley Brown made such a stink about that brought him into the sights of this disgruntled athlete was just that: his bad luck of the draw. And now they are saying that athlete you and Hurley so treasured as an all-American boy is a drug-dealing, judge-shooting mess."

"But the legislature backed me up the next time around, changing the law to require notice to parents before determining a child is an adult under the law!"

"The fact that the legislature right now in the state of Texas tightens the rules on anything is not likely to benefit the state or its people. That you helped is nothing to be proud of," Townsend says dryly.

"Well, you and me just differ on that point," Little says.

"Lay off Baker! Give the man a chance to recover." Townsend's bark is heartfelt.

"You getting soft, Jim?" Little asks.

"There are bosses over me, who don't like these innuendoes you're making about the judge and his friend."

"Well, isn't that special," Little chides, trying to sound as much like Dana Carvey doing *Church Lady* as he can.

"It's not a laughing matter to some of our people, who have the power to hire and fire both of us. Lay off Baker and do it now! Not another mention nor that you can't mention him."

"I have pictures," Little says. "I'll just switch to her."

"Give it a rest, Mickey. That law enforcement officer who watched most of that go down that night has nothing good to say about you, and he's letting the world know your version of the truth may not be so truthful."

"I sued him."

"Not the one doing the talking, Mickey. He's got a whole brotherhood behind him out there. They already know about you from your friend from some time ago who knows he saved your ass. None of them will do anything for you! That's the word."

"That was a whole misunderstanding," Little says. A local cop caught him in the wrong place at the wrong time and told Townsend rather than carrying him in; but that kindness won't happen again and now the reporter may come to know how pay-back feels.

"The luck of the draw is gonna get you too, Mickey. A lot of people will celebrate. Lay off! That is not a request... one more mention and the ride is over."

"I know. I know. That's an order. I'll think of something."

"Try not to, Mickey. Not this time."

CHAPTER TWENTY-EIGHT:
Mama in the Kitchen

"You gotta tell me this one more time, Mama," Fee Lo says, patting his mother, who believe it or not is much shorter than he and much rounder. He hugs her gently. Fee Lo is five foot nine inches and mom looks about four foot eleven inches, even with stocky shoes.

"I tell you every time, Feely, and every time you say I gotta tell you one more time. Here, I show you and this is the last time," she mocks him. Both know it will not be the last time and he will seek this same lesson every time he comes home.

"I'm ready for you, she says. "You say you're coming home, I do the beans. Here, they already soaked overnight. See how soft they are? Only happens if you soak with just the right amount of water. See they are covered but not swimming and a little bit of grease starts the seasoning."

"Okay, Mama. I get that. I fry down my fatback till it's crispy and I save that grease. I soak with just enough water to cover them and let them sit in my pot overnight."

She points toward an old Coleman cookstove that is not fully converted from wood to gas.

"Yeah, Mama, I found the stove but mine's changed over. No wood. No more. Just gas. Same color even. Red as a fire truck."

"Rinse and put more water on," she commands, and he follows diligently with her leaning over the sink as if he'll mess up even that stage.

"Peel and put the onion in," she commands. "Whole. I don't cut it up because we'll take it out."

"Garlic?" he asks.

"I don't do garlic, Feely. Papa said it made me smell."

They both laugh. Papa, his late father, sneaked and ate garlic raw. His belches and flatulence could drive the entire family from a room afterward. But he always said Mama was the one it made smell.

"Yeah, that Papa was a funny one. Okay, put the onion in whole and no garlic. Salt?"

"Not yet, the salt pork is sometimes salt enough. Wait and see what it needs. I don't do as much salt since Dr. Potts said I need to lose weight and watch my blood pressures. I always thought high means good but maybe not now."

"Good highs are something else entirely, Mama, Stay away from good highs!"

"Okay, Feely, there you go again. How is Little Pedro?"

"Little Pedro is now Old Pedro, Mama, but he's great. You know, Pedro. Always the same and always up to something."

"That's Pedro," she chuckles. "And Mrs. Roberts?"

"Mrs. Roberts is great," Fee Lo answers. "She can't hear, can't walk, can't half-see and talks in blabbers, but she's great. Still!"

"She still a *funny* girl?" Mama asks of the octogenarian, who is even older than she. She is referring to Mrs. Roberts' gender preferences.

"So far as I know, Mama." He flips his hands and shrugs his shoulders and frowns: "How would I know anyway?"

Again Mama giggles.

"Turn up the heat now Feely," Mama commands. "The beans, they need to boil rapidly for the next hour."

"An hour?"

"Yes and you have to watch them. It's the only work you have to do; but that hour of boiling breaks down the covers of the beans. The good stuff softens and comes out,"

"Mama," Fee Lo hugs her. "Oh Mama, it's so good to be home!"

"You can come back any day," she says.

"A famous man said you can't go home again," he tells her.

"You might not go back there in your understanding, Feely," she says with her typical insight. "But being there's good too."

An hour later, she orders him to turn down the heat and let the beans simmer until he is ready to eat them. Automatically, she pulls out the ceramic container of masa harina and starts scooping out handfuls into her mixing bowl for tortillas. When the dough is even, she divides it into small, round balls and sets them aside. Then she adds the masa harina again, adds flour and starts the mixing until it is fully blended for flour tortillas. Again, she divides the dough into small, round balls and sets this aside. Then she begins a masterful movement of passing each ball between her hands until it looks like a miniature pizza crust before putting in on the rack of her tortilla cooker. As the hot steamy tortillas force their way off the rack and onto the bowl that awaits, Fee Lo captures one of them and dips it into the rolling beans and eats it. He thinks he would weigh a ton if he still lived at home, and Mama cooked like this everyday.

CHAPTER TWENTY-NINE:
Packages in the Mail

"That was a very successful morning," I tell Phyll as we pull into our small parking area behind the office. "I like those people."

"They are pretty special," she agrees. "They are so enthusiastic, too."

"This may work," I say. "I thought Phoebe was receptive."

"Not her idea of a good time though," Phyll says.

"Quite," I agree. "But I think their sincerity got to her," I say.

"That's how we know there is hope for that child," Phyll says. "She knew they are doing this because they want her to succeed."

"And they are a much-needed distraction for Phoebe right now."

"That's it," Phyll says and bends down to pick up a package off the back porch where it has been positioned between two boards as if to hide it.

"I don't know what this is," Phyll says, dropping a padded envelope on my desk once we get inside.

We are both elated that our morning went so well with Phoebe, who is a smart girl and may be learning things for the first time. We are trying to utilize our group of young volunteers to make a breakthrough with Phoebe. The Judge sent her with our agreement, including Phoebe's, to a lock-down facility where she is going through drug detox as well as meeting with staff psychologists who are trying to break the ties Henry Ace Tuttle has on this child. This is not a Juvenile Detention Center, it is a very pricey place where people get the help they need at a very high price and, I think, that makes Phoebe more amenable to getting the help. Although she is kept busy with therapy and training, Phoebe has limited time to do other activities that are not part of her treatment. We are bringing volunteers who

want to support Phoebe with activities and Phyll put together   a mix
of young and older (not ancient like Phyll and I are, but not young
teens either.) They are from Phyll's Sunday school class that she has
obviously taught now for a number of years since most of their parents and siblings tell me they also went through that class with Phyll.
They are a busy group of volunteers who want to be involved and
Phoebe is responding well to them and interacting with the teen-agers
far better than we thought she would. The plan seems to be working. Part of the reason it is working for Phoebe is that Granddad is
supporting it and participating in a program for parents. It is also
bringing some healing to the family. For the first time in months, her
mother is actually visiting and mom and granddad have cooperated
on a family plan to show up at the center for family counseling.

This little group of volunteers actually accomplish more than I
thought possible and perhaps I have looked on such people as nosy
and inept and have not fully appreciated what they actually do. Twice
a year the group does missionary trips to Costa Rica and other parts
south where they have active projects going on, including building a
school in one village and sponsoring an orphanage in another.

Little did I know when I signed on with Phyll that I was getting a
dedicated activist who has more projects in the air than anybody I've
ever known before.

I pick up the envelope and examine the return address.

"Laredo. It must be Fee Lo," I say.

"Do I open it or what?" Phyllis asks.

"It says not to on the back here."

"Does that mean we can't open it anyway and see what Mr. Asshole, is up to. I can't believe he left you his fucking Harley again
and took your only transportation. And I definitely did not approve of
him permitting you to deed it over to Justin, who is in his third layer
of Nirvana with it? Phyll is on her customary campaign to stamp out
Fee Lo and his Harley. She says she hates it, but I see her hugging
Justin, a tall, muscular guy she hangs with and she doesn't look un-
happy at all.

"What is Fee Lo up to?" she asks.

"I agree he's up to something, but look at this inscription:

Confidential and Privileged. To Be Opened Only By The Court.
Somebody, somewhere has plans we don't know about yet. But I am
going to take this seriously. I don't know what he's up to, but this
is the reason we have a rather oversized safe in that storage room
of yours back there. Let's not open this. Let's put it sight unseen,
contents unknown, right there until somebody, somewhere lets us
know what he's up to. But keep the hours for billing daily; he says
we will get paid."

"Is this why you got all those subpoenas?"

"Probably, he would need subpoenas if these are what I think
they are."

"Good enough for me," Phyllis says. "It's just one more thing I'm
piling up on that man. Does he know how dangerous I am when I get
really pissed off?"

"Probably not, honey. You know how those Hispanic gentlemen
ignore what we say or do."

CHAPTER THIRTY:
Lillies in Bloom

Lilly centers her car in the driveway that leads under the pilings that hold up Judd Baker's house, careful to enter the perfect gap just large enough between the pilings to provide parking space for her mid-sized car so that she can get out of the car without standing in the driving rain.

She will wait a while to see if the rain slows down enough for her to go up the stairs without getting soaked. She turns off the car and opens the file she'd grabbed before leaving the court. So that she can work on his memory and also see how much of his prior life managed to seep through and remain in his brain despite the bullet and the surgery, Lilly has been bringing Judd problems to solve. As she starts through the motion—this one is easy, one that she has already decided to deny—that she brought to him thinking it will let her see just how much he is getting back after his surgery.

She thinks motions, such as this one to add a third party often are filed more as strategy than legal right or need. Lawyers will urge that a third party was involved in an accident and then drove off. They use that rumor to ask the court to add that person. Then they ask for a jury question that lets the jury consider if that sometime non-existent driver was at fault. They hope in that manner to spread responsibility and limit their own. Some Judges deny them as a matter of principle and Lilly studies them but refuses most of them. Judd used to laugh about them and she is looking forward to guaging his reaction to this one.

She puts the file over her head and gets out of the car.

Wet or not, she thinks, *here I come on my mission of mercy.*

On some days, being a judge is fun and like playing lawyers was in law school—things just flow because the practice is fun and trying a case is like staging a play. And Lilly loves it, being in charge. And she loves it especially when it feels like justice prevails.

The file covers her head enough for her to keep her hair dry to reach the top of the stairs when she can slip under the roof's overhang and then the porch. Knowing he will have trouble reaching the door, she opens it with her own key and walks in, calling his name. The voice she hears from a distance makes her yearn to turn and retrace her steps to the car below but it is too late for that and she gives herself the shortest of pep talks:

"You really can make a difference! Even Laura Ann said that! She has not forgotten what the physician told her months before while Judd was still in rehab and what Judd's only daughter had said.

She knows that she is having difficulty adjusting to a weakened hero. Whinny is not a sound she likes and it is made less so by her use of it with her kids: "Who invited Miss Whinny?"

"I didn't," she would dutifully reply.

"I didn't either," both kids will insist.

"Which one of us is going to tell her she has to leave?" The exercise comes full force and she hears the voice Judd has assumed too often since his injury and the surgery.

As it is, his recovery is miraculous. Always laid back, he is attractive to her because he is, face it, handsome, a distinguished grayhaired gentleman who carries his age with ease. Usually, he can see the humor she can never find in their relationship.

The assault changed him.

Six weeks since the attack, he is doing better than anyone expected him to although he is still an invalid most of the time. He has difficulty getting out of bed, walks only with a walker and at times struggles to find words to fill out a sentence. She sticks her head around the door, coyly asks:

"Anybody home here?"

"Just us invalids."

"What about that stud muffin I used to know? He ever visit?"

Judd laughs. "I'm waiting for him myself," he says, his voice lifitng.

"I stopped for sushi," she says, putting the grocery bag on the bed between them. "Shall I make coffee, tea, or me? As the Braniff stewardess used to say to you."

He smiles, a quick but still difficult response.

"How's it going today?" she asks.

"Good," he says, although he doesn't look all that good today. "On most days I remember nothing about the gunshot or surgery. Today it seeped through without my looking at those photographs on Little's cell phone. And I did get up and pick up a few things using my walker so you won't know how bad a housemate I would be."

She smiles. "That is not necessary for me, I don't clean. I pick up after the kids and I'm training them to do their own picking up. How old is Tripp now?"

"Five, I think," he says.

"We should ask Laura Ann to let Tripp and Robbie meet. They are the same age and could keep each other occupied.

"I am so tired of playing with those birds on Tripp's hand held iPad. It stresses me within five minutes. Laura Ann tries to help, but I use to play that game with that kid *ad nauseum*. Can't do it anymore, my patience is all gone."

"I understand and I didn't even have surgery. What can you do?"

"I went to play golf, which was my game!"

"You played it well. And very debonairly."

"No longer, I fear I will fall when I swing for my shot. I'm so hung up about the possible embarrassment, I can't make myself swing. The other guys are good about it. They will pick me up for the ride mostly."

"Maybe it will come back."

"Doctor says I'm a miracle, partly because that deputy pulled me out of that car fast and got me breathing. Doctor says these minor disabilities will pass as I gain strength. I lost twenty percent of my body fat and I am not good at rehab although they say my numbers are getting better.

"I do try!"

"I know you do," she confirms that for him.

"Let me get our lunch. Do you want tea, coffee, a watered down Coor's light, or dark lager?"

"You. Just you," he says, the answer she knew would come and she rewards him with a slow and long kiss. He tries to hurry things up but she pushes back and starts the kiss over with a laugh and touching the full outline of his lips with the tip of her tongue. She loves that feeling.

"I need you now," he says, but she shakes her head and gets off the bed to get their drinks.

"Doctor says mild sex," she reminds him, "whatever that is. Just take your time. We've got plenty of time for that."

"I'm a little scared," she admits.

Inside, she hopes that the reason is that, and not that she is rejecting his weakened body. And she truly doesn't know. She has done all of the things she was told would help him make progress back to his old life, which may never be possible. She has required him to start thinking by giving files with motions to consider and rule on, and they discuss them. He seems to be getting stronger.

She has bathed him, caressed him, lain beside him absorbing his warmth and gratitude at the same time. She knows she is making a difference and she plans things daily to keep him busy and keep him thinking.

She even knows that she wants him and has taken the lead a couple times to get him aroused but it must be too early because he is unable to.

She admits to herself she has to think her way to feeling the urge to go further at this point. It was such a scary thing, but he has been her soulmate for many years before their involvement ever began and she misses that as much as the parts of his personality that are seeping through recovery.

Does she just need for him to take on her problems the way he usually did and swing them away as easily as a chip shot to the green?

Is she angry because she is deep into this election now and feels that she has lost her most important fighting force?

Well, there is one thing she can surely do about it, she decides.

She takes the tray and returns it to the kitchen. When she comes back into the room, she says with a grin, "The one thing that I know for sure, Judd Baker, is that no little gunshot wound is going to bring you down. Not if I have anything to do with it."

As she talks, she reduces the light in the room and watches him as
he watches her as she removes her skirt and folds it over the back of
the chair by a small table under the windows. She takes off her blouse
and does the same with it.

When she removes her underwear, the old grin slips over his face,
the grin she likes more than any other grin in the world. He stretches
over his pillow enough to lie back and enjoy the show and he begins
to look like that debonair old fart that she loves.

It ends exactly the way he wants it to; but when she leaves, Lilly
is certain it is probably going to be for the last time until the election
is over!

CHAPTER THIRTY-ONE:
The Election Calls

When she gets out of the shower and gathers up her clothes, it is he that brings up the subject they have both dreaded.

"You're gonna get dragged through mud and worse because things are not the way they used to be when people let other people live their lives and separated stuff like sex and politics. This guy, Dickless, is on your case. He's gonna hit you with everything he can and he's already given me my hit. Tying me to you is a natural for him."

"I wish I could say it doesn't hurt ," Lilly says, "and that I don't care but it hurts every time I hear some lawyer complaining that I didn't rule right when it always seems to me the litigants that I see love me. But I never expected for people to be able to get away with what Dickless Little has done to you and is now trying to do to me."

"You do a great job," Judd says. "You're right, you're a natural at getting folks together. And you go right to the heart of the issue. You can make it over Dickless's opposition if you just don't give up. You've done nothing half the people in town don't do on a regular basis. That won't make them vote against you. You're not a crook and you're in the right party for these days!"

She draws her lips tight and tucks her chin as he has seen her do many times.

"You think the day will come when we are able to walk out that door together and go have lunch?"

"Sweetheart. I really yearn for that morning that I wake up with you beside me, right here, and when it's okay for people to know."

"I love you," she says.

"You know I love you," he says.

"There is a rumor going around that Richard is going to file to run against me on a campaign built on the need for mothers to be home with their babies," she tells him.

"I don't believe that. Richard knows better than to try that."

"I don't think he does know better. He has told me that I should go home and take care of the kids and let him replace me and for me to endorse him on that basis."

"Don't even think about doing that," he says. "Let me do some checking. It will do me good to get back out there! I never thought he was a bad man, you know."

"But the marriage is over. I knew that even more when you had this happen to you. He has finally moved out and we are doing fine together because he is looking toward his future without me. And I can't go on with him. I can't do it for politics for sure. Not for the kids, because that doesn't work. We can behave like adults. And I do love you just as it was at first."

"No," he says. "Nothing lasts that long…"

"I assume you are speaking for yourself…so yes, you are right. I took advantage of you. I never loved you, you old worn-out son-uv-a-bitch."

"That's my girl," he pats her gently on the cheek.

Lillie reaches over and pushes back the thinning hair that has fallen over his forehead. It has just grown out enough to try to control it, but it's darker and has a curl that was not there before.

"I know what you looked like as a little boy now that your hair is coming back," she teases, patting him on the head, in turn, and kissing him tenderly on the forehead. And she gets up to leave.

For some reason, she stops.

"There's nothing to be done," she says. "So don't worry about all this. I've already decided to see what happens with the election. I'm letting my hair grow a little, like you said. I bought some conservative dark suits with white blouses and pearls. You'll hardly know me the next time you see me. I guess, after the election."

He kisses her tenderly and this time she leaves, feeling better.

Judd sits on the couch counting her footsteps, twenty-nine steps that connect his deck to the ground.

So like Lilly, it is still raining but she is walking with slow, deliberate steps, so solid he can count them, and she is always more careful on the way down than up.

That bailiff saved my life, Judd thinks, *but he's gonna cost her her job if she's not careful!*

Hernandez is a proud little bastard, for sure, Judd thinks, and Judd likes him. He's made great strides for a kid from the valley. Lilly felt that Hernandez's background would make him more loyal.

"He told me to let them settle his case if that's what it took," Lilly has told him.

Judd does not believe the world works that way and wonders if it is necessary to pay Dickless some money to make him go away?

And is it right to do that when the facts and the law support that bailiff and what he did?

He looks down at his tired and wasted body and still feels the glow Lilly gave him by treating him as if he were the new man already recovered. *Mild sex,* she had said.

He smiled. *Is it time to turn tail and run?* He asks himself.

No, he answers himself, *I don't think so.*

"Hell no!" he says aloud and pushes up from the couch. He uses his walker to his room but tests the last few steps without it. He forces trousers up his weakened legs.

"I'm not about to give up that easily," he tells himself and anyone who cares to overhear. "It isn't the only thing in life that's important;, but it still is worth a damn to keep up the good fight!"

He salutes the sainted Doris as he walks by the portrait she put on the mantle. He gets his jacket on before calling Laura Ann.

"Laura Ann," he says sweetly into the phone. "Would you be a sweetheart and take me downtown this afternoon? We can take Tripp and I will buy your supper afterward."

"Oh Daddy!" she literally squeals into the phone. "You're up and you're you—just like old times. Of course Tripp and I will take you to town and let you buy us supper. Give me ten and we'll be there!"

CHAPTER THIRTY-TWO:
When Armor Feels Its First Chink

Mickey Little stretches his five-foot, five-inch frame as tall as it will go and takes off his black-rimmed glasses. He stares at Jim Townsend.

"They what?"

"It's the powers that be, Mickey, you know how they are."

"Same everywhere?"

"You might have stepped on some toes."

"You're damn right I did! I always do. That's what I'm all about. I tell it like it is."

"You tell it like *you* see it, Mickey."

"Damn straight!"

"Maybe these were the wrong toes," Townsend says. "Write a retraction."

"I won't do it. If nothing else, I am a man of principle."

"You're drawing a complaint a day from the top and it's a different owner every day. I never knew the family was this big. Your ass may be on the line this time."

"There's other papers in the great state of Texas."

"You would know."

"True, I've seen a few."

"It's just a blurb. One sentence. No one will see it. Judd Baker is not to be messed with again."

"Is he a saint? My sources say no. He fucked Lilly Pruser and bought her a bench. It's common knowledge at the courthouse that she's his woman."

"Mickey. Mickey. What business is it of yours? Some things are just that way but we don't talk about them in a family newspaper."

"Did he threaten to sue? If so, I'll write about that."

"No, he didn't threaten to sue. The man survived a goddamned bullet to the brain, Mickey. Some say that's your fault. The owners think folks are blaming the *Enterprise.* You certainly did nothing to help that judge that night. Give him a fucking break from now on. There are judges you can fuck with and there are judges you don't touch. Baker's one you've got to stay away from for now."

"Because of what happened two years ago."

"That doesn't help, for sure."

"He's ours now, you mean?"

"No, I don't mean anything of the sort. He's just done his time. He's a poor old bastard with not much time left. Leave him be!"

Little looks at the man who brought him to Galveston to prop up circulation. Gave him free reign for a pretty good time now to do his stories. Galvestonians know him, are used to him, and he sometimes makes only little bitty waves in the local water. The locals have been sanitized like CIA turncoats. Know what goes on long before the sheriff shuts things down, before Mickey writes about it. And that is only politics. Most people know whores and gambling are still the island—despite the missionary work of the Baptist and Methodists and their big churches.

City certainly hasn't shown much growth. The three sister cities, Galveston, Texas City, and League City, share little more than 50,000 each as the population settles primarily on the mainland after Ike. It was just one storm too many. Not that the old vice is gone, but some say the DA and convention center have an accord: 10 days in jail for time served and no public mention. With credit for double time, five days can be a holiday for some of those girls and boys these days.

"Never thought you'd cave," Little sneers at Townsend, who doesn't even flinch.

"Go get a beer and a hot dog, Mickey. Don't make me the heavy. I just follow orders. Put some distance on it; you'll see things differently."

CHAPTER THIRTY-THREE:
Phoebe Takes a Dive

Phoebe MacPearson stands respectfully as Lilly Pruser—Judge Pruser—walks into the courtroom still zipping her robe. She has short blonde hair pushed back somewhat in a do that would have been called a duck's tail in the fifties before Phoebe or Lilly were born. Phoebe admits it looks cool on the judge, whose hair is so short it spikes on top, just like Phoebe's.

Phoebe reminds herself of her instructions:

"Keep your pie-hole shut, little girl. Let me do the talkin'—all of it. That's what they are paying me the big bucks to do."

"You're not telling my other lawyer."

"What she don't know; won't hurt her," he says smugly. "You want out; I'm getting you out. I'm also tired of somebody else muddying up my game. You're not going to need her."

He thinks: *I'll teach that little red-headed bitch to play in my sandbox!"*

He has a plan.

Then he intends to watch that red-headed bitch stew!"

I know what to do, Phoebe says largely to herself without honoring Hurley's presence or command by sharing the thought or acknowledging him. Instead, she stands demurely beside him, while he pretends to be in control of the courtroom, its processes, the system of justice, and the entire constitutional structure.

"Your Honor," Hurley starts but the judge interrupts him.

"Mister Brown, why don't you give us all a chance to be seated and pull up the docket before you launch into your lecture on the law. We have this computer and I have to get it up and running on the right case before we can talk."

"Stand at ease," the Judge says. "At least until I get this computer up. It's slow. Doesn't want to go to work maybe."

"Okay, got you!" the judge says and looks at Phoebe. "MacPearson, Phoebe Sunshine. Set for Detention Hearing after psychological evaluation. Where is Ms. McLeod? I thought we kept her on the case."

"You did, Your Honor; but she had to be in another court this morning."

"And that would be which one?"

"I'm not sure, Your Honor; I just told her I could cover this one for her. She's still lead counsel. . ."

"Okay, everything looks complete here. Miss MacPearson, raise your right hand please. Do you solemnly swear or affirm that in the testimony you may be called upon to give in this proceeding. . ."

"Judge, she won't be testifying," Brown says, interrupting.

"Mister Brown, if you will indulge the court please, sir, I have these statutory questions that affirms the court's jurisdiction and it is in her best interest to answer those. What is your name, Miss?"

"Phoebe Sunshine MacPearson," Phoebe says as sweetly as she can manage.

"What is your date of birth?"

"April 30 2007. . ."

"Your age today?"

"Sixteen, Your Honor."

"How did it go for you at Butner?"

The judge would never see a child before her as sweet, as docile, as cooperative and as humble. Not today anyway.

"I thank you for sending me there several weeks ago now and I agreed at the time because I knew I needed what they could give me. They helped me with things I didn't even know bothered me, Your Honor, ma'am."

"Are the parents here, counsel?"

"Only counsel."

"You know how difficult that makes it for the court, counsel? If there's no parent to supervise, you know I must hold that child. I have to do that."

Indeed, he knows that, he thinks, *but wants to tell the judge just*

how hard it is to tell a MacPearson to get her ass out of bed and drive
her Sports Coupe to the Galveston County Detention Center.

And yes, indeed, he knows that without a parent, Lilly has one
choice—to hold this child again since no competent adult has appeared
to supervise any time at home.

Yes, indeedy, and he will find a way, Madam Judge! Because that
is what Hurley Brown does best, Your Honor.

⁓

"Counsel, I'm going to take a break and give you an opportunity
to notify the parents, using the court coordinator's telephone. You
might want to share with them the court's limitations."

With that, the judge turns to Phoebe: "You may be seated, Miss
MacPearson. I'll call you back up in just a little bit. Counsel, I am
going to ask my coordinator to check with Ms. McLeod about her
consent to what you are trying to do."

Before Hurley can respond, the Judge calls: "Anderson, James
Thomas.

"State's ready, Your Honor." The prosecutor is young and new.
This is his second week. His name is something like Oliver or Olivier.
He looks hopefully at the day's defense counsel: "We have a proposed
agreement for adjudication."

"Be seated, counsel, let me pull up your agreement on the computer."

"We'll waive reading of the charge again, Your Honor."

"Noted on the record."

"Do you solemnly swear or affirm that in the testimony that you
are about to give in this matter, you will tell the truth, the entire truth,
and nothing but the truth, so help you, God?"

"Yes, Your Honor."

"Are you James Thomas Anderson?"

"Yes, Your Honor," the boy says, smiling because Lilly is also
smiling at him.

"What's your date of birth?"

"May 10, 2009."

"How old are you today?"

"Fourteen, Ma'am."

CHAPTER THIRTY-FOUR:
Mopping the Floors of Justice.

Hurley Brown leans over Evie's shoulder, sniffs a little taco and body odor, and says sweetly: "Essence of woman, I love it!"

Evie pulls her shoulder away from his grasp and laughs.

"You reprobate; get your hot breath away from me before I arrest you for PI!"

"If I'm publicly intoxicated," Hurley whispers, his voice going husky, "It's with you, darlin!"

"Gotcha," she says. "Who you bringing down today?"

"You know me," he says breathing deep and expanding his chest wall. "I always have to sweep the floor with someone down here."

"I know, I know," Evie says. "We're just too dumb for Hurley Brown now in our little county. That's what you say, anyway. Hurts our feelings, you know. Being dumb and put down by the likes of you. Like infliction of a double dosage of insult."

"Present company's always excepted, Evie darlin', you're as sharp as a newly filed tack!"

He repeats this operation at the next desk, a male deputy's position monitoring those who come in for contraband in the form of knives or pistols. The deputy looks up at him. "One breath and I'll blow you away."

Hurley laughs and pats the deputy on the back. "Just seeing who came in this morning, Easy-Money."

"He's not here yet; but he will be any minute. Called twice already, checking on the judge. Talked to Evie."

"Dickless?"

"None other."

"So I wasted my time there."

"Pretty much looks like it. Typical day, right?"

"Typical day, Easy-Money, typical day for sure. Who else is on the docket? Anybody important?"

"Nobody I recognized. Don't mean they ain't important to somebody."

"All God's children, Easy-Money; all God's children. John 3:16, my man."

"That ain't what that verse says," the deputy says as dryly as he can make it, taking control of and turning his sign-in-sheet away from Hurley to face the desk. Had Hurley seen this, it would have made no difference to him. He has no problem stirring stuff wherever he goes so long as it is someone he can drop a zinger on—like this little *pipsqueak*— to the dreaded boredom of the jail before morning. Not only does Hurley Brown accept his status as a privileged BOI –born on the island—and son of a family of privileged BOIs, one of whom just happened to have been the City's mayor for more than a decade, Hurley certainly knows that he made the correct choices—he was born into the correct family and the right social level.

Following the judge's instructions, he calls mother. Then father. Then grandfather and found not one fucker within that necessary group was available for the court.

He calls mom again: Floride is a nanny who came to Galveston with a family that had been vacationing in Paris. She did the right thing in bringing her grandmother with her because the two of them fully understood the principle of using one's assets. She has done well and does not have to suffer the abuses of one Hurley Brown. "Can you take a fucking telephone call from the judge, if I can talk her into it?" he asks mother when he gets her on the telephone. The receiver remains silent for better than a minute but he waits her out: "Well?" he asks.

Silence.

More silence.

"Look, Floride-MacPearson-Stevenson-Daily-Moody-low life," he says; but when she replies it is with a voice bored and unconcerned about him or his insults. But it is serious as if she only intends to say it once: "I'm not too happy about taking her back. Call her father or his daddy and see if they can get her a hotel room and a nanny."

"Floride, are you drunk?"

"Nes pas," she says.

"How the fuck do you think I'm going to get this judge to release this child-possible-murderess to a hotel room?"

"You like the money," she says, her accent getting stronger. "Do the work."

"You're right about that, Floride, and the price just tripled. You ready for me to tell him that?"

"Tell him anything you want to, asshole. He lost power over me when I got my grandmere's money, a long time ago."

"I was sure it had all gone up your nose by now," Hurley says.

He hangs up the phone and dials his office on his cell phone. It would be just like Lilly Pruser to have the court phones on recorder.

"Miss McLeod," he tells the first recipient of his plan. "The hearing today was cancelled; wanted to save you a trip to court."

"Agnes," he tells the second recipient, "Call that Brandi Sweet, the DWI woman, and give her a new name. I don't care what it is but make it sound Baptist and deaconess-like. Tell her to go rent a suite at the Quatre Saison and charge it to us. Call me back and give me her new name and the street address, one of those back streets if possible, and do it pronto, I got to be in court in five minutes with that information."

He hangs up the phone before Agnes can grunt, much less ask questions. Agnes never asks questions anyway because she knows better than that. She's a first class paralegal and as ugly as he could find to guarantee that he never, ever, not even in a hundred years of dry would want to fuck her, although at times, she's so damn smart, he would try.

Hurley takes a deep breathe, lets it go, and smiles. He is so damn smart at times, he amazes the hell out of himself.

CHAPTER THIRTY-FIVE:
Sitting in a Morgue and Wishing I was Home

Fee Lo turns on the screen of an old microfilm machine and starts scanning another page. The morgue he is in today is in Laredo. He spent the days before in Alice, McAllen and Zapata, making his way to the border. He likes these rooms, is glad Shadow taught him what they have. She said most local papers have morgues where old stories and old papers go to die. Most have reduced these old stories to microfilm or microfiche or saved them to computers, each allowing him to clear out an issue in minutes. But Fee Lo is tired and his eyes are seeing spots and his disgust is overriding the elation of being on the right trail.

At his side is a folder thick with copies of aged clippings. He's gone through folder after folder of stories written by Mickey Little and the sickness in his stomach is real. Little has circled the State of Texas, obviously being passed on from one paper to another when he has gotten too close to getting the newspaper sued. Not that some of these stories are without value. In some, Felipe agrees with the side of the story he is being given and sees a need for someone like Dickless to have been there digging for truth, when he was. But in the vast majority of the cases, Little went against a Judge, a Commissioner, or some other public servant he got into a pissing contest with over issues that seem like little more than the person's possible slight of Little, or disagreement with the crusading reporter on an issue that probably hadn't warranted putting the public servant in the crosshairs of Little's literary gun.

Most of them look blindsided in photographs that Dickless no doubt took. They are fuzzy, half-focused, black and white figures whose eyes pop out as if hit by flares from Patton's tanks in vicious and highly inflamed attacks. Very few answered, or if they did, the answers are lost to history because Dickless never printed them.

His were one-way wars.

His suspicions borne out, Fee Lo has accumulated a longer list of people he now plans to see.

The first day home he'd spent with Pedro, the-one-Little-never-wanted-to-see-again, as Little said when he kicked the child on the street and told him to get his ass back over the river. Pedro had never been on the other side of the river. He was born and abandoned right here in the great US of A! Fee Lo met Pedro, when both were wandering in the old neighborhood. Tough, brawny, invincible, and just plain ugly, Pedro had been his best Chicano amigo since childhood. It was not the first time the two of them had conspired to protect a friend and bring down a nasty individual. The first time had been first or second grade and it had been short and sweet. Two little boys playing like thugs took on a thug, who preyed on little boys. They backed him into a corner and tricked his confession out of him by offering him sex and recording it with a tape recorder hidden in hand, no less. It was almost indecent how easy the effort had been. Of course they offered him sex in return for nickels. That being accepted by him but never performed by them, they got him on tape with the whole story. He left town so fast that they looked over their shoulders for days thinking he would catch them in an alley with a knife. Then with Mrs. Roberts' help, they mailed the tape to the prosecutor's office and the kindergarden got a new teacher.

Mrs. Roberts bought herself a new hat and wore it to take Pedro and Felipe for ice cream.

As far as Fee Lo knows, it is still their secret.

What the DA did, if anything, they never learned; but canny little Pedro survived, this foundling abandoned to the streets until Mrs. Roberts picked him up, adopted him and never bothered with formalities because she was a single woman, who liked women, they later learned, and she never tried adoption because she knew the odds were against her in Texas.

Pedro made a copy of their tape.

Or she did.

Or the new kindergarten teacher did.

Who knows?

But the old one was never seen again in the Valley. Not their part of it anyway.

Pedro went on to a life of petty crime, little things like taking change from the blind man after he played his old harmonica on the street corner. Or, watching cars for gringos on the promise their tires would not be slashed while they walked the bridge to the other side.

Probably, Pedro engaged in other and more offensive conduct Fee Lo never knew about. Pedro still held matters close to his chest. He never talked much about anything and he was industrious. His pockets were deep and stayed full and his memory was long. He sent Fee Lo to Juan Garza, the little boy they helped avoid the kindergarden teacher's abuses. Still there, he told a fuller story and Dickless Little's Story started filling out to become more complete.

Interviews were made with those whose lives Little had touched before.

Mrs. Roberts, as pale and wrinkled an old soul as you could find, patted them on the head when they reached out to say hello. She wasn't walking much these days and she had a woman from across the bridge who took care of her and kept the house where Pedro no longer slept. But her mind was still strong, and she remembered details.

The Priest would not help them.

And the Sheriff said: "Let it go, he'll hang himself and then we got him."

But Mrs. Roberts took matters into her own hands to protect the children and sent all of the information to the school board, which ushered the kindergarden teacher out of town.

Some said a nice young man lost his job.

But the little ones knew the secret.

"Somebody had to do it," Mrs. Roberts said, believing that Little had no business being around children anywhere.

And Little became the hard-nosed reporter that he is today.

Fee Lo pats the folder beside him, not feeling as complete as he thought he would feel. He reads over his list again. He has a couple of

long weeks ahead of him. He calls back to Shadow's office and asks
her for some specific documents and tells her what he has managed to
find. She understands and gets his documents and overnights them to
him, along with a copy of a letter that the Reporter had actually filed
with the Judge in the case.

Together, their work is going to prevail unless they are completely
wrong about what the documents reveal in the envelopes they will
file with the Court.

❦

The lawyer's office in Laredo is in the tallest building and at the
top, which is nothing to compare with Houston and Dallas, but it is tall
enough to make the city on the border look progressive and American,
as it faces the bustling village that lays across the river and languishes
along its muddy banks. A kid walks in as Fee Lo watches, putting his
feet in the river gingerly, going under, coming up and disappearing after
waving at the gunner in American uniform, who polices the waterside.
Water rats, they call them, but the gunner knows better than to shoot.
Fee Lo thinks of his own experience as a small boy being thrown into
his own pool and told to survive by getting to the side.

Fate served him well. He survived his childhood but there's no
way he could match this kid holding his breath. Probably, the kid has
a hidden place he can surface and then take what he can carry home
the same way.

"Deputy Hernandez," the very pretty woman who entered the
room smiles as she says his name.

"Not Deputy," he replies. "Just Felipe."

"Then *just* Tina," she says, smiling more broadly.

"The name fits," he tells her.

"He'll be a minute on the phone, then you can go in."

When she ushers him in, Felipe crosses the plush office to shake
hands with Jonas Steele and sit where Steele motions. The leather
chair is firm and doesn't sink into any kind of false comfort.

Plaintiff's lawyer, Fee Lo thinks it means knowing that plaintiff's
lawyers seem to know to have a chair that people with hurt backs can
sit in. Tall, firm chairs with support. He notes strong arms he could
use to push himself up if necessary.

"You don't have to say it," Steele says. "*The look is on your face.* Feel free. Look around you. Ask where the money came from. I don't care. Every penny spent was earned on the back of a broken-down underdog. And I'm not ashamed of it one bit. I live well and they live better than they otherwise would have without me."

"Don't need a chip on your shoulder with me," Fee Lo says. "You're preaching to the choir."

"You're right. No need to get off on the wrong foot." Steele waves one hand as if to clear the air. "You're here on the wrong mission with me. And I called your judge," he says. "She said you're not hers anymore and you're apparently no longer a deputy."

"Thanks for telling me. I didn't know how quickly they could act. Or whether they could even reach a decision together that fast. So, I'm fired, she told you?"

"No, not fired. She said you were on leave. Apparently one of your co-workers told her you were up to something."

"I am for sure," Felipe says.

"I can't help you." Steele moves his telephone from one side of his desk to the other. His movement opens the screen and he reads briefly before clicking off the iPhone.

"Hear me out first, please. I know you sued Little after he called your wife a whore. True or not, it was something he shouldn't have done, but he's not constrained by any rules of decency if there are such things. I know the paper filled itself with story after story reportedly supplied by the best of confidential informers known only to the Federal Bureau of Investigation. Said you were a drug runner, a whore runner, everything down to the lowest human trafficker pedophile, and probably because two weeks before Little started his campaign you sued a rogue IRS agent who sent his wife to the hospital with life-threatening injuries after his poor pregnant wife denied him sex. On target?"

"You know I can't say."

"Because there's a confidentiality . . ."

"You know I can't even say the word."

" . . . agreement, I know. Those things have let him get away with this and worse for a long time."

"I can't even confirm any existence of any such document if there were one; and I'm purposely using the subjunctive to say it ain't so."

"Not what I want," Fee Lo says, and then he shows him Dickless' response to discovery in which he denied the existence of any such agreements and claimed that he did not have access to any such documents held by others. And then Fee Lo shares his plans, telling Steele what he is trying to do.

By the time he makes his way back to Galveston, Fee Lo is so happy that he buys Shadow a full tank of gas, has the oil changed in her Wretched Wreck, rotates the tires and maxes out his VISA to pay for it all.

CHAPTER THIRTY-SIX:
Shadow Gets the Message

Phyllis puts the post office's mailing package onto Shadow's desk and raises her hands in surrender.

"Something tells me I don't want anything to do with this anymore than I want to keep coming to work on the back of that Harley, even if it does let me ignore the hair and professional clothing for the duration."

Her body that turns heads appears waxed over by muscle-hugging spandex leggings and she looks surprisingly good in a soft, long-line top that makes her look, frankly, twenty pounds lighter to me.

"You're losing weight."

"Of course, I'm losing weight! I can't eat for fear some yahoo is going to mow me down in an intersection and it's sex, sex, sex from morning to night from my newly christened Biker Lover!"

"You're right; that is too much of a sacrifice. Loan me Justin for a few days and I'll let him escort me around town looking like a very sexy babe with nothing on her mind but the hunk she's holding onto."

"Forget it! He already daydreams about the possibilities. But he's afraid of you!"

"We'll keep it that way," I say and wave her off and pick up the package.

"Do we know this Jonas Steele? Have we sent him business? That name sounds so familiar."

"He had some kind of lawsuit. But we haven't had anything with him. But that's the third additional envelope from the first ones. I didn't give you the two from yesterday."

"Any idea?"

"No, I called their office to see if it were misdirected and the one who answered said no, but that you would probably know it came from them on behalf of Felipe Hernandez. Same for the first two. Fee Lo's obviously busy."

"Obviously," I say, drumming fingers onto the padded mailing bag. And the other one?"

"Let me get it," Phyllis says. "These look like something we ought to put with the first one in the safe and not get our fingerprints on it."

"Got it," I say. "Follow your instinct, girl, and don't even let me see what else comes in. Just put it in the safe until Fee Lo gets back."

"Do we want to ask what this is all about?"

"I don't think so," I say. "We haven't heard of any break-ins, robberies, murders or other bad conduct from the Valley, have we?"

"Not to my knowledge; I could ask . . . ."

"Don't," I interrupt. "Sometimes it is better not to know. I have a reasonable belief that this is not contraband, drugs, or photos of where bodies are buried. Maybe that's a bit presumptuous," I say, handing the packages back to Phyll. "Don't rule out explicit photographs he's probably sending to Justin!"

"That ain't funny," Phyll snaps, leaving the room.

CHAPTER THIRTY-SEVEN:
The Other Judge

"You know what you did, doncha?"

"If you give me a hint at what you're talking about and who you are?"—*Was Susan Crazy putting this jerk through to her on the bench?*—"I can confirm or not. But who is this?"

"I'm not usually in the business of helping the enemy," Mickey Little says. "You can confirm this or not. You got your bench by screwing Judd Baker."

"I don't know what you're talking about," Lilly Pruser says tersely. "I don't know who you are and I'm on the bench with litigants before me."

With that, she hangs up the phone.

Takes a second to still her shaking hands.

Swallows.

Tales a deep breath.

Lets it out.

Relaxes.

Smiles at the lawyer standing two and half feet away and wonders if Hurley Brown set this up or heard the raspy voice or knew of it in advance since he is representing Little in his lawsuit against her.

⸙

"Okay, Mr. Brown, you've got some answering to do."

Alexandra McLeod is standing beside him.

"Judge," he says. "it's a misunderstanding and total lack of communication between me and my client. Probably my fault. I should have listened better. You know what I mean, Judge?"

"No, actually, I don't."

"It's like reading between the lines." Hurley's voice pleads. "I should have listened between the lines. You know what I mean, Judge?"

"No, actually, I don't."

"Had I any idea they were working some deal against the court, I would not have co-operated in any way. As it is, I'm a little bit caught between a rock and a hard place here. I've got my duty to my client, and I made the mistake of believing her, Judge. She's almost pathetic, you know, Judge. You can see by your own eyes, that she's just a little girl and all she's asking for is a little love and understanding. A helping hand if you know what I mean, Judge."

"Well, no, actually; the facts speak for themselves here!"

"Res ipsa loquitur," Hurley whispers.

"I know you know the vocabulary of the law," Lilly says sweetly, "I'm worried about the ethics of your situation. You led the Court to release a minor to the custody and supervision of one of your . . . other clients, this one charged with driving while intoxicated, 3rd Offense, no less; and they end up in a suite at the Quartre Saison, paid for by you."

"The clients are paying, Judge."

"And you told me this Beatrice White was a young deaconess in training at First Baptist," she added. "But that's not true, is it?"

"That's right, Judge; but that's the information I got from Ms. Agnes Tutterow, my legal assistant. I'm entitled to rely on that information."

"And it appears that Miss White's application for a name change is being held up by the District Attorney's Office because they have her under charges of DWI under a duly-issued license in that name to drive in the State of Texas under the name Brandi Sweet. They show you to be Ms. Sweet's attorney of record on the DWI. I'm not making this up, am I?"

"No, Judge. And that's what I learned myself about the same time, give or take a few hours, that you did yourself."

Hurley Brown can look so damn defeated, Lilly thinks. *Just like Adam in the garden, when being chased out by an angry God.*

"But she did this to me," *Hurley pleads, just like Adam, real tears forming in his eyes, a trick he is probably very good at, as Rosemary Brown could confirm,* Lilly thinks.

Has man not changed a bit since the creation? Lilly asks herself before turning angry eyes on Hurley.

"Do I need to call Agnes over here to straighten this out?" Lilly asks.

"No, Lord, Judge, Your Honor. Please no. That would make things so much worse, Judge. Let me work it out, Your Honor. I give you my word as a gentleman and officer of the Court that I can do so in a minute if you'll give me a recess."

"You have until I finish the last case this morning, Mr. Brown. Where is Miss MacPearson at this minute?"

"I heard that she and Ms. White were in Houston at the Galleria, Judge. I'll see if I can get them back here right now."

"I think that would work as a first step, Mr. Brown. But you might want to bring your toothbrush when you come back if you don't have it worked out. All three of you!"

"With your permission, Counsel," she says to Shadow McLeod, who had nothing to do with the subterfuge and had been ordered by the judge to take over the representation of Phoebe Sunshine MacPearson, alone, for the remainder of the case.

"Mr. Brown, I am *sua sponte*—on my own motion—removing you from this case and ordering you not to visit or talk to this minor as a sanction for lying to this court and causing this court to put a minor child on to the streets without a proper guardian."

She looks out at the patient souls in the courtroom, half of whom are snickering behind their hands. "The Court needs a five-minute break."

With that, she stands and they all stand, and Lilly Pruser walks off the bench with as much dignity as she can manage.

What do you do? she thinks. *When the people you deal with make you feel so dirty you need another shower by ten o'clock?*

She feels the heat enter as the door closes.

"Susan, I know you are mad at me for letting Fee Lo go. But putting Dickless—Mr. Little on the phone to me on the bench in the middle of a hearing... Your job is to screen all callers but no calls should be routed to the bench. You must have recognized that voice."

"Judge, I do my job. I get here early. I leave here late. I seldom leave this desk even for lunch and I cover for you while you keep your schedule elsewhere."

Susan's ringless fingers click the keyboard as she angrily brings up the docket for the next day and adds another case.

"Susan, the court's work has to go on. I've never asked you to help me with campaigning or to do anything else that is political as opposed to the work of the court and I've never asked you to cover for me when I visit Judge Baker. I am going to do what I can to help him recover, if I possibly can and I don't care who knows it. Fee Lo let his feelings get carried away. You might not like it, but I have to do those things that instill confidence that we will do our jobs. I don't need Dickless Little calling me at the bench!"

Susan says nothing.

"You know, I love Fee Lo as much as the rest of you do, and I have let him manage himself because he always seemed so capable of doing so; but he will tell you he lost it with Little and I'm paying the price!"

At this, Susan turns. Her chin tucks into her neck and her gray hair hangs over one side of her face. She looks at Lilly with disgust.

"You threw him under the bus to save your own ass and this precious job. That's what we resent. But if Dickless Little called, I didn't take the call and I don't know who put the call through to you on the bench. Maybe you better check to see if somebody higher up is pulling chains."

"You and I are the only two here."

"Yes. And I didn't do it. Maybe you should direct your anger to the person at the main phones today."

Lilly closes the door to her office.

She wants to cry because she knows Susan is right.

She did throw Fee Lo under the bus.

And she did do it to keep this frustrating job.

CHAPTER THIRTY-EIGHT:
Coming Around Again

"I've been wrong all this time," Felipe Hernandez says.

His listener raises his questionable eyebrows so high his hairline recedes, revealing how his wig is glued. Felipe had no idea it would do that under such circumstances and he laughs.

His listener laughs with him but more about his lack of belief in the honesty of Fee Lo's confession and he says so.

The real time connection is clear to Fee Lo and if he knows, Padre doesn't waver but he shifts in his seat not having the benefit of a real time look back at his caller.

"Who am I talking to here?" he asks. "This can't be the same Fee Lo I checked out just a month or two ago. And who am I to take this confession to? You've gotta be up to something Fee Lo Hernandez. This is Padre you are talking to."

"No, my friend," Fee Lo insists. "I just never saw how much I was selling out to these gringos who control our lives. But I have to. I feel like an Uncle Tom. It's a bad feeling. I was played for such a fool."

"She did drop you in the grease pretty quick-like," he says. "You got a whole courthouse ready to do whatever it takes to make sure she don't get re-elected!"

"Yeah, Padre, but I don't want that. I've just got to get my head together on this thing. Know what I mean?"

"Que sabe, amigo, but I ain't buying that you've had any change of heart. You got something up your sleeve. Everybody said you would not take this lying down."

"No. Just looking for a friend who can get a word out for me. I know you and Dickless talk. Figured you help him when you can."

"That ain't for publication, dude. I ain't looking for you to put my butt in that crack. You know?"

"I know. No problem for me. He pays well. Get it while you can."

"That ain't even a conversation that I'm having with you, Dude."

"Okay, I hear you. But I've got some stuff he wants real bad, but he don't dare call me to get it. I was thinking you could be the go-between and maybe if he likes my stuff, proof about two people he's been dying to write more about. A calendar with dates. Couple photographs. But only if you feel like passing it on and only if you can make something off it. Know what I mean?"

"I'll think about it."

Fee Lo, who has been watching this display from real time hangs up his IPhone and smiles across the desk at me.

"Son of a bitch bit like a hungry dog. He thinks people don't know he's Dickless's channel. How many envelopes did you get?"

"Seven, last I asked Phyll about it."

"That's about right."

"You got the stuff you just promised him?"

"You ask too many questions. You know?"

"Well, we have a meeting in thirty minutes. As your lawyer in this matter, it wouldn't be bad for me to know about any shi—stuff that might be dropped in my lap. Since we are negotiating."

"Don't worry, there's nothing important you don't know everything about. Did you hear what Hurley Brown did on the MacPearson thing?"

"I was there," I tell him. "He tried to drag me into it, like saying I knew about it and agreed. She laughed at him. Susan had already called me about it and I let them know I had been looking for Phoebe myself. The Clinic called me as soon as she checked herself out with her new Guardian. She laughed at him.

'I'm adding up the lies against you, Sir. I believe that's another one,'" she said.

"She did not give him the time of day and threw the book at him. He is off the case. Apparently, she can be brave when it counts for her. She sure held his back to the wall."

"Most lawyers don't tell bald-faced lies to the judge," he says. "That's all people will talk about for two days but it will die.

"That so and so," I say. "He is as coated in Teflon as Reagan was. Let's get going, please, I'd rather have the advantage of being early than late."

CHAPTER THIRTY-NINE:
Why Bureaucrats Have a Bad Name

Brett Rutter arranges files on his desk in a way he thinks looks busy. The County is providing Felipe Hernandez with representation—but not the regular employment lawyer, who is one of the few in the section that can actually try a case. Brett Rutter, no relationship to the family that started the oil and chemical business, but he will have folks think he is, is a friend of the County Attorney, who come spring, will take a leave from his public duties, i.e. kissing up to the commissioners on behalf of the County Attorney, to set up the campaign office and start acknowledging the contributions as they slip into his pocket daily for just the type of favors that Brett grants freely to someone as soon as it is decided what the county's response will be on such things as contracts. Co-counsel, when chosen, charge mighty amounts and never hesitate to consider settlement using the taxpayers' money.

On the safe side, Brett contacted the other side in this case and, just for grins, talked about the likelihood of an offer to Little, through Hurley, that he could maybe get in the 750 range.

Seven hundred fifty *thousand*, that is.

And, although he reports that the Commissioners are not thinking of this case as more than a near miss, they see the chance here to do right by Dickless. *He'd have to be careful not to mess up that way*, he reminds himself. *He's heard that Dickless can be somewhat sensitive about the nickname.*

If he's peeved, it's justified, Brett thinks.

Shouldn't happen to a civic-minded soul like that reporter. Keeps them all straight, is what he does.

That's my position and I'm sticking with it, Brett mumbles to himself with a smile.

This is what you do, Brett, he reminds himself. *Let's keep it straight.*

Now, to break the news to Fee Lo and get that lawyer off his back. Who does she think she is? Threatening Brett and the County Attorney!

Threats!

A lawsuit! Against him and the CA personally for failing to supervise Brett!

"Based on his favorable treatment of Dickless," she says, he's laid the groundwork for her! The nerve! He might have to teach that Bitch a lesson!

He leans back in his chair and puts his feet up as if he's been working all morning to get this worked out for everybody. About the time he gets comfortable enough to nod off, he hears their knock on the door. Standing quickly, he almost knocks over his chair and does knock over one of the stacks of files that fall off his desk and spreads out across the office.

They fall in front of and in the way of two chairs he placed in front of his desk to direct them to. He bends over to pick up the files and hears and feels a seam in his pants rip and pop open, no doubt exposing his rear. Caught that way, Brett kicks the files beneath his desk and quickly returns to the safety of the side of the desk with which he can hide at least the most embarrassing part of his problem.

Unfortunately, the whole episode causes him to start sweating profusely. In these lean days of working at the Courthouse, he has put on a little extra weight, which he will lose as soon as the campaign starts. He never stops then, for sure, and knows the success of the campaign always depends on his efforts and has little to do with his boss's glad-handing.

For one thing, the CA is no campaigner.

While Brett, the son of a former Justice of the Peace, was weaned on pressing the flesh! So to speak.

&

"Mr. Rutter, it's so good to see you again," I say, although he cannot possibly remember where he's seen me before because he probably hasn't. Kissing up is all I'm doing to put him off his guard.

"You, too," he says, shaking hands with first me and then Fee Lo.

"Too bad about all this, Deputy," he says, waving with open hands as if to look more accessible and sincere. He's too fat to pull it off and sweat is rolling down his face and dripping off his chin. You can almost sense his butt cheeks are clinched since he's not breathing.

"You can rest assured this County's representing you, Deputy. We take care of our own. When it gets close to trial, I'll take on co-Counsel to assist me—maybe even this lawyer of your choice—but we'll go after this bastard. That's what we will do."

"Then we need to talk about this letter that Mr. Little insists that you sent to him," I say, passing across the desk a copy of a letter Little had indeed sent to my office in acknowledgment of my claimed representation and Little's insistence that my help is not going to be needed since he has settled the case.

"As a matter of fact, Mr. Rutter, Deputy Hernandez has both a legal defense to this case as well as a belief that certain evidence that he's been able to gather will give him an important victory in this case."

Rutter settles into his chair, struggling with what must be a line of sweat beads running down the indentations of his spine. He appears to be doing a new seated dance. I guess we would have to call it the *errant pee sensation* dance.

Meanwhile, I'm thinking: *You lie like a big dog*, but I hold my peace.

Caught in the lie of his settlement offer in the letter to Little, I can tell he needs time to calculate a decent response.

And I don't intend to interfere with that mental effort, because I want to see just how quickly he can save himself, if he can; and I know there will be no settlement anyway without a big load of caca hitting the proverbial fan because I brought a sack full of it with me and intend to rub his nose in it if he takes another step to settle this case.

"Uh," Rutter starts several times but is totally unable to go forward. A mouth breather apparently, he closes his fish-like mouth, opens it again for air and goes through the process over and over, uttering not a word.

"Briefly," I finally say. "As long as the officer has a good faith belief that his reasonable suspicion is correct, the United States Supreme Court gives leeway to protect the arrest, although this was clearly not an arrest for the commission of a crime. Deputy Hernandez not only had a good faith belief that a crime had been committed—Judge Baker was right there in his car with blood oozing from a gunshot wound to his head! Deputy Hernandez, despite Mr. Little's interference, held the Judge's head above the ditch water and used his own body to crawl out of the car supporting the injured Judge. He is a hero and you are going to pay this 'bastard' as you call him 750,000 dollars? That's outrageous.

"In addition," I quickly continue, "he could not see the gunshot wound at first because Mr. Little leaned into the car, blinding the deputy with his camera's flash and preventing the deputy from carrying out his rescue.

"We agree that Mr. Little told Deputy Hernandez that he had seen what happened, but the story of some unknown vehicle he claimed to have seen at the scene, and for which he had a tag ID number by photograph, could have been viewed as far-fetched since this reporter has a long history of dislike for this very judge. He did nothing to help this judge despite his obviously perilous condition. Deputy Hernandez told Mr. Little to step away so he could continue his rescue effort—which he did by the way, inching the Judge from the car, clearing his airway and administering CPR until the Judge was breathing. And Mr. Little interfered at each step and did nothing to help. And you want to insult this officer by paying this worthless reporter $750,000. That's truly outrageous!

"Fortunately," I continue, "all of this is on the Deputy's vehicle camera! We agree that Deputy Hernandez put Mr. Little into his police vehicle and he was not free to go. The deputy seized his camera because even Mr. Little contended it contained evidence of the crime. And though the photos are of extremely poor quality, the camera running in the squad car the entire time shows Mr. Little's obstruction, his disrespect for the officer, his unforgivable racist taunts. And it was Mr. Little carrying on a dialogue; he spoke but the officer never asked him a single question. There's not a jury, court, judge or appeals court that will find a single thing wrong with Deputy Hernandez's conduct that day. And you want to pay this man $750,000! That is truly outrageous!

"Does it strike you as strange that the *Enterprise* has non-suited its earlier claim and published an editorial based on interviews of its readers who found it ridiculous that this reporter would seek damages when there can be none? It called the Deputy a hero and wished him well in the future.

"Does that strike you as strange? Isn't it the newspaper's right under the first amendment and doesn't this say that the newspaper finds no loss of its constitutional rights by conduct of this deputy?"

"And does the state's right to the evidence of the attempted murder of its Judge mean something to the public? And you are spending the public's tax money to the tune of $750,000. I hope the public lets you and the county attorney and the commissioners know how outraged the public is at the way you throw their hard-earned tax money around."

"Little, even if what he says is true—which is absolutely not true as far as this deputy's conduct is concerned—if he saw what he says he saw, he identified himself as a material witness in an attempted murder case. He was held for his own protection. If he saw what he says he saw, the driver of that truck was still out there and still armed and probably knew whoever was in the reporter's car, saw it happen. He could have come back. Can Little carry this first amendment case forward against this deputy on his own? He is not the press. Once he claimed the camera recorded a crime, he described himself as a material witness with proof to support his claim.

"We would suggest that the state has an overriding right to the evidence—especially when, as here, the District Attorney downloaded it and returned the camera and copies of everything to the newspaper's lawyers, who didn't seem all that aggrieved or interested in taking custody of it."

As I talk, I watch Rutter go from interest to confusion.

He has no idea on earth what I am talking about. Hadn't thought about it! I have heard that he prides himself, in fact, on being able to resolve cases irrespective of the merits. Brags about it, in fact. And he is not only the highest paid employee of the county attorney, he does his own work on his own cases contemporaneously with his time for the county.

What a life!

"Well, of course," he finally says, when I stop to catch my breath.

"I'm glad you agree," I tell him sweetly. "Because if you were to attempt to follow through on this letter to pay Mr. Little seven hundred and fifty thousand tax dollars to settle this worthless lawsuit, I'm afraid Deputy Hernandez is going to sue you personally for making the implied admissions in this letter which are contrary to the facts and are a threat to his future employment with the county or others. Your willingness to sell him down the river this way despite your false promise and your duty to defend him, which you even repeated when we came in your door today shows bad faith, malice, and dishonesty with your employee! It is certainly actionable and maybe we will just ask for $750,000 also.

"Deputy Hernandez puts you on notice he will seek discovery of who authorized you to send this letter, which would be valid only if the commissioner's court has already voted and agreed to it. And we will sue that body and each of them. And if no commissioner authorized it, Deputy Hernandez will sue you and the county attorney.

"It that all clear, Mr. Rutter?"

Rutter sits silently.

"Very," Rutter finally answers. "I was just buying a little time for the deputy with Mr. Little. That's the only reason I sent the letter."

"Mr. Rutter, do you make seven hundred and fifty thousand dollars a year?"

"My pay is public record."

"I just wonder how you came to throw such amounts around so casually," I say, standing and leaning across the desk to hand Rutter the second letter I brought. "That's a lot of money."

"This letter—mine to you and several others—memorializes the notice I've just given you in this conversation," I tell him. "I took the liberty of mailing a copy to the county attorney, and each member of the commissioner's court, along with a copy of your ill-advised settlement offer and why we oppose it."

"There was no need to do that."

"I just wanted to make sure that it didn't get lost. You've got a lot of files piling up under your desk there. You're working too hard!"

❧

"That lard-ass!" Fee Lo explodes as soon as we get back in my beat-up LeMans. "He was getting ready to sell me down the river!"

"'Fraid so," I agree. "We're gonna have to watch him like a hawk. I sent a copy of his letter to the county attorney and commissioners. Figured they might want to know what he's trying to do with their money— especially since it's before any time that they could have agreed to it!"

"Felipe Hernandez," a tall-good-looking young man that I've seen before, but not for a while, says as we walk up to my building. He points papers in my direction; but Fee Lo reaches out his hand and interrupts the delivery. "I'm Hernandez, I remember you, dickhead!"

"He said giving it to the lawyer was good enough! Described her pretty well too."

"I'll take it," I say. "If Little's doing his own case, maybe I can find a defect or two in this." I wink at the process-server, and he returns my wink with a smile. A very nice smile that makes me feel surprisingly good.

"Won't bother me none," he tells me, touching his brow in salute.

"God, I love what the military does to a man," I say to him in response to the salute, feeling his reluctance to let go of my hand after holding onto it just a little too long. I smile.

"We met before," I say. "But I've forgotten your name."

"Oh yes," he says. "Didn't think you'd remember."

"But I never forget a pretty face," I say and we both laugh. "I guess you're back in town," I add.

❧

"And I thought you were ice," Fee Lo says after the process server leaves. "You were all over that guy!"

"I was not," I say. "You jealous?"

"Hell no. I know your kind. You'd coldcock that guy like lightning if he really came on to you!"

"You don't remember the night you and Bubba and another guy pulled me out of the Bay?"

"That was him?"

I nod and he looks at the US marshal's disappearing back.

"I thought that guy was an agent, FBI or something. He's just a marshal?"

"Maybe a disguise," I say, grinning.

Fee Lo looks down at his papers.

"Is this what you told me Dickless would do?" he asks pointing to the papers.

"Yes, as soon as you told him he could throw the settlement letter away for all the good it would do."

He nods.

"Right as rain," I say. "He dismissed the county suit in state court and re-filed in federal court; because he knows the gig is up. His own paper abandoned the suit and wrote an editorial calling you a hero! He wants to drag it out by adding a 42 USC 1983 case saying you violated his personal civil rights."

"Did I?"

"I don't think so. He's just paying more filing fees for nothing now."

"Aren't you even a little afraid?"

"No. Federal judges are stronger than God; and they never have to run for election. That means that neither the religious right nor the Tea Party nor any other special interest group can ever threaten them into submission. This Judge is special anyway. He's young. He's new. He's feeling his oats. In fact, he has a good kind of arrogance and still thinks he can do good and change the world. I would have a real crush on him but for the fact he has a wife and eight children."

"Wow!" Fee Lo says. "Busy man."

"You just have to file more paper in federal court to keep them happy. And fast. But we're ready, Fee Lo. Don't worry. You're gonna have fun with this before it's all over."

"I ain't having fun yet!"

CHAPTER FORTY:
The Judge/The Newspaper

"Look what it did for Bill Clinton. Does he look hurt?

Townsend leans way back in his chair till it squeaks to tell him he's gone far enough. He holds Baker with a level and incredulous gaze.

"Okay, you made your point," Judd says, but privately, he thinks what happened to Clinton may have helped Trump in 2016.

Townsend isn't usually one to put his feet on the desk, but he does this time because Baker has his on the other side of the desk.

"They actually said this was good for the circulation in my legs. Elevation. Works somehow on swelling." Baker explains because he would never have done that before his injury.

"Well, do what they say. You always think they know what they are saying anyway. I don't know about your friend and how this will affect her. We've told Little to lay off. He's got multiple ways of getting it out there."

"It's your business that's gonna hurt if she files a suit against you for something you can't possibly have proof to support."

"He says he's got something coming. I got a hint it might be somebody close enough to keep a calendar or take pictures."

"No, he thinks it's coming from Hernandez," Baker counters. "I'm not gonna say anything bad about that young man. He saved my life. Did everything right. Little's wrong on this."

"I know," Townsend admits. "That's why we're not in it. Little's a fool sometime. The DPS officer at the scene came to see me. This is not for publication, but he said that deputy went beyond duty to make sure he got your head out of that mud. He slid you out of that car and gave you CPR til the EMTs came and took over. Then he got you on the ambulance and sent that officer with you to make sure he could tell the hospital people who you were and what happened to you. There was no waiting for you, sir. You had first class, Grade A, medical treatment right here on this island. And that deputy was the one who did it for you!"

"Little's bit off more than he can chew with this one."

"I agree with you. Little's a fool," Townsend says.

"But he's your fool," Baker reminds him. "Seems we were doing okay before he came along. If you can't reel him in a little, no pun intended, he is gonna keep stretching the truth the way he does. Lilly is going to do what she has to do as well to win this election. She has this one chance."

"Truth is a defense," Townsend says.

"Since when does truth make a difference, Jim?" Baker asks, his voice rising.

"We washed our hands of it. He's gonna print it in the paper or on his blog that will be picked up by other papers."

"So you won't lose, breaking the story," Baker says.

"It's not that cut and dried, Judd. Readers have come to expect something like that from him. Circulation is up, and I don't think they have that many illusions about what he tells them."

"So that's what it's come to," Baker says. "What happened to us, Jim? You've been here as long as I have. This island used to be a pretty peaceful place to live. And fun. Is it worth it? For circulation?"

"There are always younger editors out there preening about what they can do if given a chance. Every business has its rain-making department. Courts too, old man, you're not immune from this. Your friend is part of that younger age. She doesn't look like a judge of the old tradition."

Baker laughs. He enjoys the image of Lilly's punk hair and her unconventional look. She sure didn't look like a judge, he's right.

"I'll give you that," he admits. "But what are we doing to our civilization in the long run if we do away with the tradition and heritage?"

"I think it might have started with Nixon," Townsend says. "Firing Cox. Going through three AGs before he got one—do you realize it was Bork that did that? Fired Archibald Cox as Independent Prosecutor because he would not let them tell him what to do. Folks said that is why Bork lost his Supreme Court nomination."

"I didn't know or don't remember," Baker admits.

"Really took off in the nineties. Newt's social compact was nothing more than an agreement to add slash and burn politics to the system. You can't get a decent candidate to even consider doing the things you have to do to run for anything. Can you believe some of those assholes? I was almost glad about Trump because he moved Cruz off the top of the ticket."

"I washed my hands of politics when I retired," Baker confesses. "Just stayed around to do visiting because it is so much fun just to do the work and not have to answer to political demands. I like that part best."

"You understand the public's pretty gullible," Townsend says.

"Oh, I know."

"If he paints her as your whore, it's gonna be nasty. Doesn't matter about you. I can see it your way. Good-looking young woman gives an older gentleman the favor of her body. Nobody would expect you to say no. No reason prevents it. But she's technically still married and even if they are separated, she has two young kids to set an example for. She might be a creature of the millennium, but most voters aren't. Little says one of those kids is yours."

"God damn," Baker says. "He is a bastard. But that is not even possible. Had those things clipped a long time ago and I can get the medical records to her if you go there."

Townsend smiles. "Those were the days," he says. "I never minded poking it just for fun."

"Can you endorse her over Little's opposition?"

"Probably, but we'll all have to keep an eye on him. He editorializes in everything he writes and he says things I worry about. I think his days are numbered. It's just when it catches up with him."

"Even journalism is changing," Baker says,

"Oh, yes. When I started out, if you mentioned yourself, John King Sr. my editor at the *Dallas Morning News* scratched the story. Today, we send them out and the story is how they got the story or not. I doubt we'll go back to the old tradition because everyone is concerned these days with self. It starts and stops with self."

CHAPTER FORTY-ONE:
Old Cases Reignited

"You blow oxygen on a dead fire and it sometimes sparks," Hurley Brown sputters.

"That's the kinda homespun reasoning that seeks to avoid the issue, son," the caller says.

"Well, I'm not avoiding anything, Joe. I represented that kid two years ago when he tried to stop his girlfriend from killing his baby!"

"That ain't here nor there," the caller says. "He's done tried to bring about a killing himself and he's lucky that old man up there with his head shot up survived it all. He's going up if it's the last thing I do while I'm in office. You're not gonna shoot a judge on my watch, I don't care what you think that judge did. Hell, this might get me re-elected, and I wasn't really counting on it."

"Nobody's gonna run against you, Joe."

"Those days are over, Hurley. Everybody gets an opponent these days. And they run with pride. As if they know how to do the job they're seeking when they don't know enough to find the right courthouse. One of them newly elected Tea Party women went up to Austin looking for Nancy Pelosi. 'I'm new' she said, and 'the first thing I told people I would do is let Nancy Pelosi know her days were numbered. I got some things to say to her. Right now!'"

"'Well,' the guard told her. 'You're gonna have to go to Washington, D.C. to do that, ma'am.' And there is no political chivalry left anywhere."

"You got that right, Joe. Guess I'll be talking to you."

"Not so fast, my man," the DA says. "Word is, Hurley, that if I go over to that warehouse you store files and things in, I'm gonna find a beat-up pick-up truck with a license plate that begins TLC. And it belongs to your client little Henry Ace Tuttle, one-time star player for Ball High, who just can't seem to make it happen on any other football field. He's been a first-class pain ever since graduation with a bad case of *you owe me* for the world."

"He's messed up. That's for sure, Joe."

"And you've been covering for him because he helped you and Dickless Little burn Judd Baker's ass when he said that little girl was old enough to make her own decisions about what she wanted to do with her own body. And the boy had no say. I never understood what that was all about, Hurley. Dickless is kind of asexual 'cause even a blind man won't have him; but you probably been spreading your fertile seed all over this town you been at it so long."

"It's the principle of the thing, you see, Joe," Hurley says.

"It was the media glare, Hurley. Don't think you're gonna fool an old man this late in the game. I never saw what threw ya'll for such a loop."

"That did get so out of hand," Hurley agrees and sits quietly, scribbling a note all the while to Agnes Tutterrow to send Able out to the warehouse and tell him to dump that you-know-what into any canal deep enough to sink it in. He knows the next question before it's asked because Joe asks it every time that he has Hurley's cross-hairs in a bind.

"What did you say ever happened to that girl?" the current district attorney asks.

"Her parents sent her as far away from Texas as they could get her until the distance washed Henry Ace Tuttle and his you know what out of her system."

"Now what's she doing?"

"Graduate school or some such somewhere in Europe learning about art!" Hurley says.

"Well, good thang for her," Joe Boyles drawls; and, as if he'd forgotten entirely why he called the errant lawyer, he starts to hang up the phone. "Oh, by the way," he adds, "I got cameras set up on that storage building of yours. Anybody tries to mess with my evidence is gonna be in big trouble."

The line goes quiet.

Hurley sits tight.

Crushes the note he wrote to Agnes and throws it in the trash. Closes his eyes till they hurt. Frees his mind of all complications. And it comes to him as it always does: A brilliantly calculated solution.

 He is full of them.

"Agnes!" he yells. "Get me the number for that new girl over at the *Enterprise*, I need to do some justice here. Do it yesterday!" he commands.

"Sugar Doll," he says as soon as Cleopatra Jones answers. "Are you ready for your first big scoop?"

His busy mind doesn't even register her answer.

"Well, I've got the story of the year for you; but you got to come over here to get it. Bring your photographer 'cause I'm gonna let you do the discovering of somethin' ever-body's been lookin' for in this town and that nobody could find."

He'd show Joe Boyles what happens when you try to drop turds in Hurley Brown's sandbox!

CHAPTER FORTY-TWO:
Breaking News!

Breaking News, Channel 13
This just in from Cleopatra Jones, Reporter from *The Galveston Daily Enterprise:*

> *Good afternoon in Houston, Dave, I'm here in Galveston, Texas, where the Enterprise just discovered the battered pick-up truck driven by a hit and run driver, who left former District Judge Judd Baker in dire circumstances without offering aid after shooting and running the highly respected jurist off the roadway in the early morning hours. The judge was leaving an emergency hearing at the Galveston County Detention Center.*
> *Thanks to excellent medical attention at the Sealy Hospital in Galveston, the judge is recovering from serious injuries after taking a bullet to the head.*
> *This lady beside me is Miss Agnes Tutterrow. She called the Galveston County Sheriff's office to the scene. Miss Tutterrow is the legal assistant to well-known attorney Hurley Brown. Miss Tutterrow went to the Brown Law Office's storage room this afternoon to retrieve a file and discovered that the storage room had been broken into at some point and the vehicle believed to have been driven by one Henry Ace Tuttle had been hidden inside the storage room. She reported to this Reporter that she called the Sheriff immediately to come to the scene of her find.*
> *Hurley Brown, a well-known Galveston attorney, told the* Enterprise *that he was immensely proud that his legal*

assistant knew exactly how to handle the incident and that she had done the right thing. Tuttle, Brown described, was a former client but he reports that he has not seen the young man in about two years. At that time, Brown filed a lawsuit for Tuttle to get a restraining order against Judge Baker to prevent his order permitting Tuttle's similarly under-aged girlfriend from being certified as an adult for the purpose of letting her obtain medical treatment for a pregnancy she alleged resulted from Tuttle's rape of her.

Reporting from Galveston, Texas, this is Cleopatra Jones, Reporter for the Galveston Daily Enterprise."

Cleo takes a deep, deep breath and smiles over at Hurley.

"Thank you, Mr. Brown. It went exactly the way you said it would. I've never been on TV before. I'd like to talk to Ms. Tutterrow while I have my cameraman here about any other story in there about how this all really came to be?"

"I don't think so, Darlin, but I would be honored if you would permit me and my lovely wife Rosemary to take you and Ms. Tutterrow to dinner tonight at the Galveston Country Club, assuming you're not about to go to dinner with me by yourself."

"That assumption is correct sir, but I have to take a raincheck anyway. My paper just texted me that the Today Show called and they want an interview. I'm going to New York City tonight! I'll be on the Today Show tomorrow morning. You really know how to set things up, sir!"

The girl runs to her car in excitement and Hurley enjoys the sight until she drives away.

"Sometimes, Hurley," he tells himself, talking to the open field, hands held wide in amazement. "You are so smart, you amaze even me!"

"You amaze me too, Hurley," the gravelly voice of the local DA says as he crosses from the curb to where Hurley is standing, watching the girl drive away.

"Joe," Hurley says and pops the District Attorney on the back.

"Mr. Brown," the DA says. "In all fairness, sir, I am putting you on notice; you're being watched."

CHAPTER FORTY-THREE:
The Gig Is Up!

"Your Honor, we are here on a motion to compel the discovery of what we believe is the production of relevant documents. We are not asking the Court to hand them over to us. We are asking the Court to order the plaintiff, Mr. Michael Little, to be required to produce these documents, under seal to you for an *in camera* examination by the Court or its appointed Master in Chancery.

"We have good reason to believe that the evidence will show that Mr. Little engages in the same type of behavior involved in this litigation before the suit recently filed in this Court. We believe that the evidence we are seeking will show a pattern of behavior that is abusive of his role as an investigative reporter and will establish that he participates in creating his own emergency and then blames it on others and seeks a monetary reward. This goes beyond investigative reporting to malicious invasion of privacy, harassment, and extortion. In the past, as he did in this instance, he masks his criminal conduct as the work of a journalist. He invades the lives and privacy of public figures, and seeks to extort damages, which he does not accrue as a result of any conduct by them in order to carry out a false charade of charges. In this specific case, he caused this deputy, a hard-working public servant, to unjustly lose his job and to suffer personal embarrassment and mental and physical anguish by bringing a lawsuit challenging behavior by the deputy that was not only constitutional but demanded of him due to Mr. Little's attempt to destroy the scene of a crime. In addition, at the scene of a horrible attempt on Judge Baker's life, Mr. Little impeded the investigation of this deputy into what had happened and claimed personal knowledge of what happened to the judge. He threatened, he failed to assist, and in fact he abandoned the judge, who was gravely injured by a gunshot wound to the brain and instead invaded the privacy of the judge to take numerous photographs of him in that grave condition.

"By engaging in such conduct and insisting that he saw the crime against the judge occur, he forced Officer Hernandez to place him in protective custody in order to preserve the scene of an attempted murder. He then sued on his own behalf seeking to extort 'damages' from the deputy and his employer.

"We sought these documents in discovery, Your Honor, and Mr. Little filed no objection and made no response to the discovery request. He has, however, stated to the court in an *ex parte* letter that, I quote: 'There are no such documents.'

"That statement is false. Because the court accepted his letter as a response to discovery, we also believe that Mr. Little knows that such documents do exist and he has been for some reason disingenuous with the court. Privilege may not be used affirmatively to conceal improper conduct and it may not be used to protect a lie or a crime and should one try to do that, the privilege is waived.

"Your Honor, these documents should be produced and reviewed *in camera* by the Court to determine if Mr. Little attempted to hide behind some claim of privilege. Such conduct waives the privilege.

"Your Honor, Mr. Hernandez spent several days researching this matter and I would ask the Court to permit me to call him to make a showing of good cause to Order the Production."

"You may call your witness," Judge Raleigh ruled.

"I object, Your Honor."

"On what legal grounds, Mr. Little?"

"Freedom of the press."

"Thank you, Mr. Little. Overruled. You may call your witness."

"Defense calls Felipe Hernandez, Your Honor."

"Mr. Hernandez, do you solemnly swear or affirm that the testimony that you may be called upon to give in this proceeding will be the truth, the whole truth and nothing but the truth, so help you God?"

"I do, Judge."

"Counsel, do you want him in the witness box or standing here?"

"Standing here is fine, Judge. We'll be very quick." I am happy to be at the bench because I want to see Mickey Little's face as the questions and answers are given. He's less than three feet away, and I can feel and hear his breathing.

"Mr. Hernandez, give the judge your name for the record please."

"Felipe, F-e-l-i-p-e Hernandez, H—"

"I know who you are Fee Lo, I can fill in that part," the reporter says. Everybody smiles, including the judge because she thinks the court is hers!

"What part of the state are you from, Mr. Hernandez?"

"The Valley."

"What part of the state of Texas is the Valley in, Sir?"

"The South quadrant and points further West."

"When were you there last?"

"I've been there, except for a meeting here, for the last four weeks at my mother's house."

"And why?"

"Judge, this seems to me like a waste of time," Little breaks in.

"It's very relevant, Your Honor. I'm about to make that clear."

"Do so. Despite our interest in knowing more about Mr. Hernandez' origins and his mother's hospitality, we do have limited time." The judge is new. He's still feeling his oats, also his power.

"What did you do there?"

"I visited with my good friend from kindergarten and we, Pedro and I, went to see a former victim of this plaintiff, John Garza. Both asked me to extend their thoughts to him."

"And what next?"

"I went to the newspaper morgues where Mr. Little worked and read as many of his articles as I could find."

"And what next?"

"I identified at least six other cases that he filed for money damages in as many counties from people working for the government that he disagreed with on some matter or the other."

"And what did you learn?"

"That all the cases were dismissed at the end by final judgment."

"And what did those judgments say?"

"Isn't she supposed to have certified copies of those judgments, Judge, if she's gonna talk about them?"

"I think that's an objection, counsel, that I can sustain."

"Thank you, Your Honor. That leads me where I am going. Your Honor, we have what is marked as Exhibit A, 1 through 7. These are stamped with the certification of each of the district or county clerks who placed the documents under seal. With each is the subpoena authorized and signed by this Court."

"Your Honor, I have an objection. It is clear from a quick reading of each of these that they don't say anything at all. They certainly don't say how the case came out."

"If I may ask the witness another question, responsive to the objection, Your Honor: Mr. Hernandez, did you learn anything about the actual disposition on these cases?"

"I did."

"What did you learn?"

"All seven were settled with a confidentiality agreement the parties kept."

"And did you learn what was in those agreements?"

"I am sure interested in hearing that answer, Judge. Looks like I'm gonna have to sue seven people all over again," Little says, interrupting.

"You may answer the question, Mr. Hernandez."

"I got the names of the lawyers and asked them to honor my subpoena to produce copies of any documents that matched the description that Mr. Little answered falsely by saying there were no such documents; and I asked them to put any such documents under seal and send them to my attorney's office so we could give them to the judge to inspect."

"How many responded to the subpoena?"

"All seven."

"Do you have these with you here today?"

"I do."

"I want to ask you a question about each one of them and then I will ask you to hand it to Judge Raleigh."

"Was this document sent to you under seal and is that seal still in place?"

"Yes, it was, and the seal is intact."

I repeat the question for each of the seven. The judge hands each to Little to confirm that he knows what is being submitted.

"Mr. Little, am I going to discover that these documents are probably documents that you have copies of, or the ability to obtain copies from the lawyer representing you or your paper?"

He mutters an affirmative answer that takes almost as long as the Judge's question.

"Is that all, Counsel?"

"Yes, thank you, Your Honor."

"Mr. Little, do you have anything to add?"

"Your Honor, would it be possible for me to meet with this woman and the deputy?"

"I don't know what that would accomplish, Mr. Little. I am sure you want us to do justice for you in this case. We've put you on the trial docket preferentially to get your case to trial today."

"I just think I can save the court a lot of time and you're busy here."

The courtroom is in fact full of spectators, who have come from all over the courthouse system because they trusted their belief that Fee Lo never takes anything lying down and that he always has something up his sleeve. Most of them have not had such entertainment since the time two criminal lawyers played out their lusty divorce case over the course of two days in which they did everything but sell peanuts and beer to their audience. Most of the spectators are courthouse regulars and know exactly what confidential settlement agreements are. If anybody paid, it was the newspaper that let Mickey Little run wild from some dispute he had about some public official he either disagreed with or just used to stir up trouble.

"Do you two want to meet with him?" the judge asks.

"We are willing to talk, Your Honor, but I don't think we are going to waive our discovery dispute. I brought the court an order, granting the motion to compel."

I slide the order onto the rail around the Judge's bench and give Little a copy at the same time.

"Then I make a motion, Judge," Little says. "I nonsuit this case with prejudice to refiling it here. I have no interest in trying to get justice from this court and, in fact, I don't think I can anyway."

Little throws the order granting discovery back at me and stomps out of the courtroom to a spattering of applause.

"Order in the Court. Ladies and Gentlemen, you know you can't do that," the Judge says, stacking the documents to one side. "I'll wait until five o'clock to give him time to file his paperwork before signing this. I've got plenty of other work to do. This matter is in recess until five o'clock," he says and bangs his new gavel.

"Next case, CV-16-1826, Button v. Briggs. Come on up Counsel."

CHAPTER FORTY-FOUR:
The Brewery

"You know I don't drink beer," I say, "But I love the atmosphere in this place."

"It's over?" Fee Lo asks.   "I ordered you a Pino."

"It's over because he nonsuited with prejudice. That means he can't file it again, not here nor anywhere else."

"I want to buy you a hamburger too then, since you're telling me you had so much fun, you're not going to charge me a fee. I think we've seen the last of Dickless here, anyway. It's time for him to tuck tail and run."

"It's never over, Fee Lo. He will rise like a phoenix every time he wants to cause someone a little misery. It may be over here for you."

"I don't think it's just that, this time, Miss Shadow. You are real smart, but you don't know everything. I'll bet you ten dollars his paper will announce tomorrow that some paper in a galaxy far, far away has lured Dickless to their staff and although the *Enterprise* will miss him, they wish him well. The people of Galveston will miss him. But most of them have already opened up the windows and doors to clean out the very smell of him from their life.

"He will hold out his chest in bombastic pride at being sought by yet another fine establishment in Texas, or whichever state is lucky enough to receive his eminence, and he will ride into the sunset on that golden steed from which he seeks justice: *Victory! Freedom of the Press!* And the only soul who will be truly sad to see him go is poor old Padre, whose milk money is slipping out the door with its tail tucked between its legs."

By the time he finishes, I am laughing. Phyll and Justin are bending over laughing and Fee Lo bows expansively to his audience, which is clapping and laughing and yelling Whoop! Whoop! Many of them followed Fee Lo to the brewery after the courtroom denouement.

"What is this about him not paying us?" Phyll asks.

"I was told to submit a voucher. I don't know how generous it will be, but it will be something. I'll work hard on everything else the rest of the week."

"I know you will," she says. "Sorry, the Grinch in me came out!" We both grin.

Fee Lo puts an arm around Phyll's shoulder. "You know this pretty woman ain't broke, Miss Phyllis. IF she wants to do the Lord's work for free, you should sit back quietly and let her do it. I promise you your heavenly reward for taking care of a lost soul like me will be great. I'm alone! I lost my job. I had to give up my house. I'm sleeping in one of those little bitty rooms with really bad beds."

"Don't go on. You know this woman would die of starvation before she'd tap into any available help!"

"You're taking advantage, Fee Lo, like you do with every woman."

"Justin, how'd you let this woman get so riled up, my man?" He hugs Phyll affectionately. "She needs an attitude adjustment more than any woman I've seen in a long time."

"Maybe I should borrow the Harley for another week."

"No!"

"Aw, come on Phyll, be a sport!"

"This is fun," I tell them. "But we are due in court tomorrow on Phoebe's case. We need to be ready. It's a big day for her."

CHAPTER FORTY-FIVE:
Justice for Phoebe

"What are we doing on it?" Fee Lo asks and Phyll's eyebrows reach her curly hair that's a little windblown but makes her look younger. She is having a hard time adjusting to *our new self-appointed partner*.

"We worked out an agreement with the state—or at least with Olivier, but we haven't heard the last of Bennett, I fear... Her grandfather endorsed it and her mother agrees to it. First time they've had that much harmony in years. And Phoebe is ready."

"That is the good part," Phyll says. "We've got a whole Sunday school class of volunteers to give credit for that.

"I agree," I say. "It certainly helped that they formed that group and started making those visits. Phoebe knows there are people who care for her and support her and want her to succeed."

"And Phoebe is going to get the help she needs," I add. "Willingly!"

No one can deny the occurrence, I think. *My little client killed another child in a state of uncontrollable anger while under the influence of a hefty amount of drugs.*

While that is not an excuse and a crime was committed, prison is not the answer. Detention, a 14-day process, is not the answer. And I have no idea what the state will demand when we come together again; but today I am going to argue for recovery. She has a problem. She doesn't really see what it is yet; but Dr. Godfrey believes she can face it and deal with it. I can only hope for the future.

But she can still face jail time.

Phoebe is still a juvenile.

She was plied with drugs by a young man who is actually worse off than she. He definitely doesn't see it and is refusing care.

Although he still denies that what he did was trafficking, she was also trafficked and convinced that hers was a love relationship with him. She did things to please him despite the fact she said it was painful. I believe he doesn't really like girls and he punishes them for existing. What he does to them is totally unforgiveable as far as I am concerned because it begins with control. Once he has them sufficiently pumped up on drugs, he uses them, then he passes them on for a slight fee, of course, and they are too knocked out to realize it.

I had no interest in working this case when it was first assigned. Now, I have seen a world I had no idea existed, and I do care. Again, I recognize the benefit of having a protective mother and think all of them should be that way. But it will never work out that way. Too many parents believe children should experience disaster and learn their lessons. But some people, it kills.

Phoebe was a child reared with money and privilege but in fact, she was as bad off as the child without anything. I have not found one person in her life who provided her with real love and guidance.

I know it is actually Phyll that Phoebe calls for guidance and she respects Phyll just as Phyll's Sunday School Class respects her and I am so proud to stand in my paralegal's shadow in this way. Phyll is a really solid and great person who cares.

Phoebe's grandfather agreed that we should stay on as her lawyer until we get her out of therapy and although he doesn't speak to me in the hallways, suggesting he doesn't know me from Adam, it satisfies Phyll's demand that we consider bills for at least some of the work we do.

And I guess Fee Lo has become an associate, of sorts.

"Come on," he says, signing the bill and taking my keys. "Let's go make sure Phoebe is still on the program. I'll drive."

≈

The next morning, Phyll pulls out my best voir dire suit. Although I know we are not asking for a jury, I want my client to think I look like a proper lawyer. And I want to honor the judge who is coming in for this hearing. Over the months since this case started, we have had many other cases and worked many other angles, while he has done one: recovery.

I was warned by Lilly Pruser that he might stumble but this was the most important thing that we can do for him because he remembers my *little girl* and her problems and wants to be involved.

He has not given us an indication of what he will accept but the door is open for me to ask and the State has agreed to certain terms.

I stand for the judge as he comes into the courtroom, that same makeshift room in the Detention Center. He walks slowly and with a cane, but he is on his own feet, crossing to the bench.

We are all there.

My client and me.

Deputy Fee Lo Hernandez, the former chief deputy of the court, now a legal assistant who sits with me at counsel table.

Deputy Ismael Pope, Fee Lo's replacement.

Evie, who brought in the juvenile alone because she is now fully cooperative and dressed in her own clothes.

William Catherton Bennett, who takes the State's table alongside Olivier, the newcomer. Olivier has a few more months to grow in the job and Bennett has moved up to the felony bench. He still insists this case should come with him. He also is eager to start the process of certification; but by now he must know that this judge is no pushover.

Judge Judd Baker calls the case and asks the State to call its first witness.

"We have none, Your Honor. We rely on the record and ask the court to admit it and consider the facts for themselves. We offer the record for sentencing," Bennett says. This is customary; the state has done its job.

The judge calls for the juvenile's first witness.

"Miss MacPearson calls Dr. Betty Godfrey, Your Honor."

William Catherton Bennett rises. "Your Honor, we object to the calling of this witness. We have no evidence of any expertise that would suggest any value to her testimony."

"Your Honor, with all due respect to Mr. Bennett, he has not given us a chance to speak and lay the predicate for her testimony; but I have Dr. Godfrey's curriculum vitae and have previously provided it to the State. He also has been given her academic record, her publications and the history of her having testified and been accepted as an expert on behalf of our children in some 250 cases in this area alone." I hand the court what I referenced so he can see each case.

"Let me take a look at this," the judge says and I am so happy to hear that voice of his. "It might save us a lot of time," he says. "She is or she isn't. Stand at ease, please."

I wait, knowing this judge has found this woman to be an expert before and that he will do it again because nothing has changed.

But we wait.

After a while, Judd Baker looks up and I see a pained expression and then I understand. There must be a deficit. I ask Fee Lo to access the Center's computer and print a list of her cases on which Baker has accepted her testimony and there are 50 of them. He obviously is recovering from his injury by working with the Juvenile Court.

"Your Honor," I say. "Former Deputy Hernandez printed out the list of cases in which you have found Dr. Godfrey to be an expert. May I approach with the list?"

Bennett looks like he's been hog-tied and I don't know how long he will suffer in silence; but the child's grandfather has now quietly taken a seat on the back row of chairs. I notice that Bennett looks at him and knows full well who he is and whose side he is there for.

I smile.

If Mr. Bennett has one talent, it is responding in a manner that is politically appropriate if a little obvious and lacking in professionalism.

We all wait patiently, first for Fee Lo, who approaches and gives me the original to hand to the Judge and he hands over a copy to Bennett himself.

"The State withdraws its objection, Your Honor. You have indeed found this witness to be an expert on what looks like about 50 of the 250 times in which she has testified and it looks like a majority of those were testimony for the State. The State accepts the witness as an expert."

"Counsel," the judge says, looking at me. "You may proceed."

Dr. Godfrey takes the stand, a chair in the wing of the bench rail and she looks comfortable and at home in her black testifying pantsuit as he administers the oath.

The reporter tells the judge she is ready.

The judge nods his head at me, which tells me I can proceed.

"Dr. Godfrey introduce yourself, please, to His Honor."

"Dr. Betty Godfrey, a licensed child therapist."

"Do you know Phoebe Sunshine MacPearson?"

"Yes, I do, and I know her very well at this point." She makes eye contact with Phoebe, who smiles.

"We will talk about how you know her, but first I want you to tell the judge how you came to be a licensed child therapist."

"I earned my degrees at Baylor College of Medicine in Houston, Texas. I qualified for my license largely doing undergraduate and graduate work at the University of Houston and working for the courts and for the Texas Department of Health and Human Services and for the Children's Protective Services."

"Given the papers provided to me, I am going to shortcut this by finding that Dr. Godfrey is an expert and that her opinions are reliable," the judge says. "You may continue, Counsel."

"Did I ask you to review the records of and to visit with Phoebe Sunshine MacPearson?"

"Yes, you did."

"And what did you do in the way of research before meeting with her?"

"I talked to family members. I read her record with this court. I read the charges against her and I also read the available file (which means I did not get it all) but I needed to know about the young man that was there on the evening of the event that led to charges. I then reviewed the materials I try to familiarize myself with for every case involving young people. I also met with Phoebe and I believe that we are communicating well at this time." She makes eye contact with Phoebe, who smiles.

They did not get along at first.

"I spent 16 hours with her in consultation and lately she has agreed to meet me occasionally for ice cream. She has a large number of friends there and I have to actually get in line." Again they smile at each other and I silently thank Phyllis for her class.

"Did you reach any conclusions to support a recommendation to this judge as to this child at this time?"

"Yes I did."

"And what did you decide?"

"I found a child who came under the influence of an older young person who has in fact lost his way and I have serious questions about his future. The relationship matured into one of psychological master and a dependent, made willing to do whatever he required her to do to maintain the relationship. And the drugs," she adds.

"And was there a source you found for that?"

"In my opinion, this child has been sexually trafficked by a manipulative person who should be removed from society. The incident that gave rise to these charges resulted from his having abruptly taken her from his favored placement and assigned her to subordinates to satisfy. This conduct was designed to increase his control over her and to make her more compliant to his demands and to acknowledge taking on a new role in which she is likely not to survive. The confusion resulting from her treatment and the new regimen of drugs set off the anger that she was simply unable to deal with. I fear he is branching out into an even more dangerous area."

In fact, I know that Dr. Godfrey has talked to the state about these activities, in confidence, but that nothing has been done about it. This is information I will use if it becomes necessary in the future.

"The good thing about that," Dr. Godfrey says and there is literally a drawing in of breath throughout the courtroom. "She is ready to deal with this and, in fact, has developed good friendships where she voluntarily committed herself for help. "

In fact, the night after the Pruser hearing in which Hurley Brown was removed from the case, Phoebe voluntarily returned to the Clinic.

"She has found a supportive placement where trained professionals deal with this one day at a time, and it takes time. It takes so much time."

"Do you have a recommendation at this time?"

"I would leave this child in her present placement until she and the staff jointly believe that she is ready for another evaluation. Under no circumstances should there be an expectation of less than one year. The problem is severe because the young man was her primary source of love and he is still attempting to make contact with her and to persuade her to leave her placement and return to him. It makes her more aware of her aloneness and she is struggling to cope with the isolation she feels by being separated from him. But she is ready to work at it. I also recommend that procedures be initiated to place him under a no contact order for her protection."

"Thank you, Dr. Godfrey. Your Honor, I pass this witness."

William Catherton Bennett rises from his chair and I expect a few questions. Personally, he wants jail time. He still wants certification; and it looks as if he is winding up to sling a hardball at Dr. Godfrey, but he does a surprising turn-around.

"The State has no questions, Your Honor."

Judge Judd Baker accepts Dr. Godfrey's recommendations by signing the document handed to him by the State's attorney. I notice that he reads it before signing. I have also received a copy and know it is the agreed language, or I would object.

A chair slides behind us and an elderly voice speaks. "Your Honor, I respectfully request to have the record show that a family member is present for this child's hearing and that the family member is humbled by what he heard about what has happened to this child. I won't seek pity by saying we did not know and never dreamed such a thing could happen in this community and in this country. But we would ask for consideration by the good doctor and ask that she make some time on her schedule for an old man who sees for the first time that he has to learn all over again what it means to be a parent in our times. We have obviously failed this precious child and I wish to offer my cooperation to make it right for her."

I sense as much as see Phoebe turn to look at her grandfather.

I don't believe she knew before that time that he was here.

～

My friend, it's good to have had this time with you. Much of this is second hand, I know, but my life is beginning to dance to a lot of different drummers and I had to gather this together by gleaning through lots of gossip.

Fortunately, courthouses are perfect places for gossip and second-guessing, and I did a lot of that when I started telling you what I think is on their minds. You'll have to forgive the parts where I had to make up what they were thinking; but the way things work around here, I think I probably came pretty close to getting it right.

Thank you for asking about this courthouse since you know I'm spending quite a bit of time here. It isn't like any other that I work in. It is not fancy or old or traditional, it has no plastered walls or highly polished marble floors, but I love going to work here anyway. Long use is making it real (Just like that rabbit you and I used to read about as kids).

Real courthouses are old and sagging and mysterious and stand like monuments to the law in the center of town. What could be bad about that? And I get paid to work. It's not a lot but it pays my part of the bills.

The one outstanding thing about courthouses is that wonderful people work there.

I'll write more when I have time, but in the meantime, keep painting, sculpting, walking in the desert and all those wonderful things your life consists of! It always shocks me that you want to hear about my life when yours is a virtual paradise. I love the last painting you sent me a picture of. I have a lawyer friend here that saw it and I think she wants to buy it if you put a price on it.

Oh yes. Please don't forget to tell Clarice I love her when you see her next. You know, now that I have a kid looking to me for guidance, I see things a little differently about my own Mother's overprotectiveness. And I worked up the courage to do what you asked. I went by the rehab place and visited with Bobby Gene. Grace was there and true to her name, she made it a lot easier for me to accept that after looking for my father all these years, I don't get him until he is in this state. I don't know if I can make that visit again, but Fee Lo says he is here and he will go with me and that might help. I'll talk more about them if I can the next time.

Bye now, and love, Shadow.

photograph by Sonya Cuellar

CAROLYN MARKS JOHNSON has an eleven-book series about the Courthouses of Texas and the stories that flow from them. The series starts with these two, *Detention*, and *Rutter Industries*. Carolyn loves her work in the legal field but is an artist and writer. She was a reporter-photographer for newspapers in Austin, Dallas, Raleigh (NC) and Greensboro (NC). She won awards for investigative reporting.

A student of history, she held a Research Fellowship from the Lyndon Baines Johnson Library in Austin and studied in the Presidential Papers of Lyndon Baines Johnson, which provided the basis for her Master's thesis: "A Southern Response To Civil Rights, Lyndon Baines Johnson and Civil Rights Legislation 1957-1960 (University of Houston, 1974). She holds a Master of Judicial Studies Degree from the University of Nevada's National Judicial College, writing, "Juror People Preferences, A Houston Jury Project."She taught History and Government at Alvin Community College (1974-81) and at the University of Houston as a teaching fellow (1972-74 and teaches 'Voir Dire and Jury Communication at South Texas College of Law (1998-Present). As an undergraduate at the University of Houston, Carolyn took Fourth Place in the Atlantic Monthly's nation-wide Literary Contest (1972); and the Louis Kestenberg Award for Outstanding Graduate Research Paper.

Printed in the USA
CPSIA information can be obtained
at www.ICGtesting.com
LVHW040415130924
790711LV00002B/7